Love Burning Bright

Love Burning Bright

Angela Elwell Hunt

Tyndale House Publishers, Inc.
Wheaton, Illinois

Dedication
For the staff of Camp Kalagua . . . with thanks!

Library of Congress Cataloging-in-Publication Data

Hunt, Angela Elwell, date
    Love burning bright / Angela Elwell Hunt.
        p. cm. — (Cassie Perkins ; #6)
    Summary: While at Camp Katumba, a church camp in North Florida,
Cassie falls in love with a reckless boy who wants her to compromise
her Christian values.
    ISBN 0-8423-1066-5 :
    [1. Church camps—Fiction.   2. Camps—Fiction.   3. Christian life—
Fiction.   4. Florida—Fiction.]   I. Title.   II. Series: Hunt,
Angela Elwell, date, Cassie Perkins ; #6.
PZ7.H9115Lo   1992
[Fic]—dc20   91-42891

Printed in the United States of America

99 98 97 96 95 94 93 92
 9   8   7   6   5   4   3   2   1

Important People in My Life, by Cassie Perkins

1. Glen Perkins, my dad. ♥♥♥♥♥
   He used to be a systems analyst at Kennedy Space
   Center, but then he moved to work for NASA in
   Houston, Texas. Even though I don't see him
   much, I think he's the most handsome, talented
   man to ever walk the earth. *No one* can make lasa-
   gna like he can.

2. Claire Louise Perkins Harris, my mom. ♥♥♥♥♥
   She's an interior decorator and now she's married to Tom Harris, a lawyer. Mom had a baby
   a few months ago, and she grumbles a lot about
   being too old to change diapers. It's not that she
   doesn't love the baby, it's just that she's tired
   a lot.

3. Stephanie Arien Harris, my new baby sister. Or
   half sister. Whatever. ♥♥♥♥♥
   The latest addition to our family, baby Steffie
   looks like me and screams like the devil when
   she's not getting attention. She'll probably be
   spoiled to death.

4. Max Brian Perkins, my brother. ♥♥♥♥♥!
   Max moved in with us when Dad moved to Houston. Max is the only eleven-year-old in the tenth

grade at Astronaut High, my school. He's a genius, and he has epilepsy, which scares me to death, but Max deals with it. He says a lot of geniuses have had epilepsy.

5. Dribbles, my Chinese Pug. ♥♥♥♥
She's still just a puppy, but she's growing. Tom got her for me the day my old dog, Suki, died. I love her, but honestly, she can be a pain. She's eaten two pairs of my shoes and my favorite purse and three of my favorite cassettes.

6. Chip McKinnon, my boy-friend. ♥♥♥
I write it like that because he's a boy who also happens to be my friend. Chip's cute, funny, and best of all, dependable.

7. Tom Harris, my new stepfather. ♥
I hated him at first, but a lot has happened since then. Lately I've realized he's really trying to do what's best for all of us in this new family. Tom is OK, even though he's nothing like my dad.

8. Nick Harris, my new stepbrother. ♥♥
Nick's in eleventh grade at Princeton Academy, a snooty prep school, and he's really into sports and cars and all that stuff guys like. I used to think he was *really* cute, but since he became my brother, he's just ordinary.

9. Jacob A. Benton, or Uncle Jacob. ♥♥♥
   He still won't tell me what the *A* stands for. He
   lives with us, and he's gruff and tough and runs
   the house. I really like him.

1

I wasn't surprised that Tom, my stepfather, wanted to get rid of us. After all, Mom had just had a baby, and taking care of little Steffie wasn't easy. Plus, Nick (my stepbrother), Max (my brother), and I seemed to always have something going on, and Mom and Tom and Uncle Jacob were a little worn out from chauffeuring us to science fairs, choir concerts, and basketball games.

Tom made his announcement at dinner. He stood up, cleared his throat, then he spoke in his lawyer voice: "Attention, please."

We all stopped chewing and looked at him. Even Steffie stopped waving her fork and throwing peas on the floor.

"Next month, you kids have your spring break."

"Are we going to the beach?" Nick asked. "Everyone else is."

"No," Tom said, glancing at Nick. "And please don't interrupt. Since you kids have a week out of school, it's only fair that your mother and I have a spring break, too."

Max's left eyebrow shot up the way it always does when he senses something unusual is coming.

Nick grinned at his dad. "It's OK, Dad. Just rent us a condo on the beach and we'll stay out of your hair. You can send Uncle Jacob to cook for us—"

"Hold your horses," Uncle Jacob interrupted. "I've got plans for that week. I'm going on a cruise to the Bahamas." He rolled his eyes and waved his arms in a crazy imitation of a hula dance. I couldn't help laughing even though Tom was trying to be serious.

"No, I'm not renting a condo and leaving you three unsupervised," Tom said, shaking his head. "And I don't want you hanging around here because your mother will spend all her time cleaning up after you. But I was talking to that guy down at the church where Cassie likes to go—the guy who works with the kids—what's that guy's name again, Cass?"

"Doug Richlett," I answered. Doug was my youth pastor.

"Right. Anyway, he's having a spring camp for teenagers that week and I'm sending all three of you. Richlett said it's at a really nice camp and I know you'll all enjoy it." Tom sat down. As far as he was concerned, the matter was apparently settled.

Nick groaned. I knew the idea of going to church camp didn't exactly thrill him.

"Don't worry, Nick, I happen to know that some of the kids from your school will be at this camp, too," Tom said, passing Nick an extra-large helping of Uncle Jacob's out-of-this-world cherry pie. "And the food's good, I hear. You'll have a great time."

"Camp?" Max looked at me and crinkled his nose. "Are we talking 'roughing it'? Are we talking outhouses?"

"It's not rough at all," Mom said, wiping Steffie's face. "In fact, Max, you can probably find all sorts of experiments to do out in the woods. You'll be surrounded by wildlife."

"Wildlife." I closed my eyes and thought about all the horrible stories I had heard about camp . . . toilet seats smeared with Vaseline, girls' bras flying up the flagpole, rising at the crack of dawn to stand in a drippy, dewy three-mile line for breakfast.

For weeks I'd been looking forward to spring break, to lying on the beach and soaking up some sun. But now, instead of smooth sand and a golden tan, I'd be hiking through the woods, covered with mosquito bites, scared to death that under every rock or leaf was a deadly snake. Oh yeah, it was going to be a great spring break.

I looked up at Mom. "What are you and Tom going to do?" I asked.

"Nothing," Mom said, smiling at Tom. "We're going to stay home, watch reruns on television, swim in our pool, have Chinese food delivered every night, and see absolutely no one."

"Except Steffie," Tom added.

"Right," Mom said, nodding. "Except Stephanie. Taking care of her won't make me so tired if I don't have to take care of the three of you, too. I want just one week to relax."

Brother. I'm surprised they didn't send Stephanie off to camp, too.

Chip called later that night. "So you're going to Spring Camp?" he asked, his voice cracking in excitement. "That's great! I went last year and it was super. Camp Katumba is really nice. There's horseback riding, swimming, canoeing, the blob—"

"The blob? That's not something we eat, is it?"

Chip laughed. "No, it's this thing in the water— you'll see. It's all fun. You'll love it."

"Well . . ." I hesitated. I still wasn't sure about this camp idea, but if Chip was going, at least I'd have someone to hang around with. I knew Nick wouldn't be caught dead with me. And as much as I like Max, hanging around with your eleven-year-old brother isn't much fun.

"Come on, Cassie," Chip said. "Where's your spirit of adventure? Trust me. It will be a week you'll never forget."

"OK. I guess it'll be fun." I was beginning to feel better already.

After thinking about it a few days, I was pretty excited about Camp Katumba (where do they get these weird names?). I talked to some other kids at school who'd been there, and they all agreed that it was a nice camp. "It has the most important thing," one girl told me. "Air-conditioned cabins."

It was beginning to sound better and better. Life at school had become so boring—the same classes, the same teachers, the same homework, day after day. Now that our few cool days had passed, the sun was shining brighter than ever, and I could hear sea gulls laughing outside the windows of my school. I wondered more than once what would happen if I got up in the middle of class, walked outside, and never came back.

It's not easy to live in Florida when you're surrounded by tourists on vacation. In the grocery store, while Mom and I are loading up our cart with regular stuff, there are people in shorts and sunburns who giggle and load *their* carts with hot dogs and hamburger and buns and suntan lotion. They wear Mickey Mouse caps and have bumper stickers on their slow-moving cars that tell the world they've been to Gatorland, the Reptile House, Sea World, and Cypress Gardens. While they're having all that fun, we regular people poke along behind them, going to school, going home, and dreaming about being free to go outside and goof off.

I was bored, bored, bored, bored, bored, bored, bored, bored, bored—and in a rut. My best friend, Andrea, was still going with Eric Brandt, which meant she wouldn't be my best friend for a while. I can't stand Eric—he thinks he's too cool for this earth, and he's mean, too—but I can't say anything against him if Andrea's around. Chip, who used to give me goose bumps just by walking by, is more like an ordinary friend now. He calls me and we talk a lot, but that's about it. He spends a lot of time working at his uncle's veterinary hospital, too, so he's not around much. I'm proud of him for having a good job, but he doesn't have much time to do things with me. I guess you could say our relationship has cooled off.

So maybe camp would be fun. It would be nice to be in the woods instead of on the beach. Chip said the camp is in north Florida, where the nights still get cool and the trees are oaks, not palms. If I stayed home, I'd just have the same old beach and the same old sand, so maybe tall trees and cool nights would be a nice change.

That's what I told myself anyway. I mean, it's not like I had a choice. Tom had already filled out our registration forms, paid our camp fees, and signed our emergency medical releases. We were going to camp whether we wanted to or not.

2

On the last day of school before spring break, Chip
met me by my locker. "I'm sorry, Cassie," he began,
his face a mask of disappointment. "I hate to let you
down."

My stomach knotted. "What's wrong?"

"I can't go to camp."

"Yeah, right." I shook my head and smiled at him.
"You're kidding, right?"

"No, I'm not." His blue eyes were serious, and suddenly I realized he wasn't pulling one of those sick
jokes guys find irresistible.

"Brother." I slammed my locker and turned to face
Chip head-on. "Why can't you go?"

"My uncle's lab assistant got sick and had to go
into the hospital. So there's no one to help him with
the animals that are boarding, and there are more
animals than usual coming in next week because of

spring break. He asked me to help, and I think I should." He shrugged and looked down at the ground. "It's my responsibility."

"But you had plans! You're already registered for camp and everything!"

"That's OK. I know Doug will understand. But I feel bad, Cass, because I know I told you I'd be going."

Great, I thought to myself. *I could have invited Andrea to go along, but no, I thought Chip was going to be with me all the time and I didn't want Andrea to feel left out. But now it'll be me who wanders around alone.*

"It's OK, Chip," I muttered. "Go take care of your dogs. I'm sure they need you more than I do."

"I'm sorry, Cassie," Chip said, reaching for my hand. "I promise—I'll write you, OK?"

"Sure." I took my hand away and pretended to straighten my books. My voice was as flat as I felt: "Have a great week."

Tom and I waited in the car for Max to get out of school. Tom was excited about his week away from the office, and he rattled on about the cases he'd postponed, the settlements he had been able to reach, and how wonderfully efficient his secretary had been to clear his calendar.

"What about you, Cassie?" he asked, turning to glance at me over his shoulder. I was in the backseat, trying to ignore his jabbering, but his question brought me back to reality. "Oh, I'm fine," I answered lamely. "I didn't have much of a social calendar to clear."

"I mean, are you excited about camp?"

"Yeah." I stared out the window for Max.

Tom sighed and turned away, and I felt a little guilty for being so moody. My bad mood wasn't really Tom's fault.

"I just found out Chip can't go to camp," I said, trying to explain. "I just wonder if I'll know anyone there."

"Of course you will. You'll know Max and Nick." I made a face, and Tom laughed. "I know, brothers aren't the same thing as friends. But, Cassie, I know you'll make new friends. Camp is a great place to meet people."

Maybe. I saw Max then and shifted my books off my lap for the ride home. Why didn't Max hurry? I hadn't even begun to pack, and we were being shipped off in less than two days.

Max came toward us slowly, as if the sun were draining him of his energy. At one point he stopped, covered his eyes with his hand, then he suddenly slumped to the asphalt parking lot. Tom and I both stared in stunned silence, but as Max's body stiffened, I cried, "It's his epilepsy! Quick!"

Tom and I flew out of the car. Within a minute we were by Max's side, and within two minutes, Max's seizure was over. He was drenched in sweat, and a few curious kids had gathered.

One girl stepped forward and saw Max. "Grr-oss!" she squealed to her friends.

"Get out of here!" I snapped at her. "Leave us alone."

Tom carried Max to the car and I followed right behind them. Max hadn't had a seizure in months, and we were both surprised and caught off guard by this one. There was no way I was going to let my little brother become a public spectacle. I was glad Tom was there. He buckled Max, who was weak and pale, into the seat belt, then drove us home. It was all over in less than five minutes.

Max told us he hadn't been taking his medicine. "But honey, you've got to take your medicine," Mom said, her concern showing on her face. "What made you think you could stop taking it?"

Max shrugged. "I thought perhaps my condition had progressed to the point where I no longer needed it," he explained. "Or that perhaps a lower dosage would prove to be sufficient."

Mom rolled her eyes. "Max Perkins, no matter how smart you are, you're not smarter than your doctor," she scolded. "And you're not to experiment on yourself by not taking your medicine, do you hear? Agreed?"

Max nodded. Mom looked at Tom, who looked a little pale himself, then she looked back at Max. "I don't know if I should send you to camp," she said slowly. "If you were to have a seizure at camp, Cassie might not be nearby to help."

Max snorted. "I'm not going to have another seizure, Mom. I said I'd take my medicine and I will. You don't have to worry!"

Dummy Max. Mom was offering him a chance to stay home, and he wouldn't take it!

"Cassie, will you try to keep an eye on him?" Mom was looking at me now. Her eyes were worried, and I found myself nodding. I knew I could have used Max's epilepsy as an excuse for both of us to stay home, but that wasn't really fair to Mom and Tom.

"He'll be fine. Don't worry," I said, echoing Max. "Everything will be fine."

Mom nodded, a little reluctantly, then she stood up and left Max's room. Tom stepped forward and rumpled Max's hair. "You really scared me there, ol' buddy," he joked. "I didn't know what hit you."

Max ducked his head shyly. "It's nothing," Max said. "A lot of geniuses have had epilepsy."

"Well, it may be nothing to you, but it was

something to me," Tom said. His eyes were misty. "For a minute there, I thought we were going to lose you."

Max just smiled and looked embarrassed, but I took a mental snapshot of Tom rumpling Max's hair and looking scared. Maybe Tom did want to send us to camp for a week, but he definitely *didn't* want to get rid of us. That was an oddly comforting thought.

Nick missed out on all Max's excitement, but he had troubles of his own. He was in the kitchen when I came downstairs, drinking one of Uncle Jacob's specialty Coke floats. Uncle Jacob was wearing his tell-me-all-about-it look.

"I just don't get it," Nick said, pounding the kitchen counter. "I bought the girl flowers and sent her a teddy bear. Isn't that what girls want? I try to be nice to her, but honestly, Uncle Jake, the guys who lie and cheat on their girlfriends seem to have it better than guys like me."

Uncle Jacob leaned forward on his elbows. "I don't know girls today, Nick," he said. Then he saw me. "Cassie, what do girls want? Nick says the old-fashioned things like flowers and candy don't work anymore."

I shrugged. Chip had never really been the flowers and candy type—I don't think he could afford things like that. Nick, on the other hand, could buy a girl anything. "Maybe the girls know you're rich," I offered. "So buying them stuff doesn't mean much. Maybe this girl you like would appreciate something you really worked on, like a poem or something."

Nick snorted. "I've tried that. I wrote Jacklyn—" He bit his lip. He hadn't meant to tell me her name. "Anyway, I wrote her a letter. I worked on it all night, and the next morning after she read it, she still ignored me. I just don't get it. I mean, I have this friend at school who's a real jerk when it comes to girls, but the girls are always after him."

"What does this guy do?" I was curious.

Nick gave me a disgusted look. "You don't want to know. First, he talks about *everything* he does on his dates, things I know the girls wouldn't want talked about. When he goes out with a girl, he just sits in the car, honking the horn for her to come out. He asks girls to go steady and cheats on them. I hear girls say they can't trust him, but they'd do anything to go out with him." Nick shook his head. "And here I am, a nice, ordinary guy, and my dad taught me to go up to the front door and meet the girl's father. I think it's wrong to lie. I'd never cheat on Jacklyn if she'd go out with me."

"You're boring, Nick." It slipped out, and I didn't mean to hurt his feelings, but I could tell from the look in his brown eyes that I'd hit a sore spot. I tried to soften the blow: "I mean, you're too predictable. Maybe this Jacklyn wants some excitement in her life. Try being spontaneous sometime. Pick her up and go on a picnic, or dedicate a song to her on the radio or . . ."

I drifted off into my private ideas about what would be romantic. I used to write romantic things in my private notebook and wonder why Chip never came up with any of the same ideas—things like riding bareback together on the beach under a full moon, or jumping off a yacht in evening wear and going for a midnight swim. Chip would never think of those things. He'd think I was crazy for suggesting them.

I frowned as the idea struck me—Chip was a lot like Nick, only he wasn't rich and he never spent hours writing me letters.

Uncle Jacob offered an idea as Nick slurped up the last of his Coke float. "If you have to change your image to get a girl, maybe she isn't the girl for you."

"I don't know about that," Nick said, winking at Uncle Jacob. "You haven't seen Jacklyn."

They kept on arguing back and forth, and I stopped listening to think about Chip. He never did anything romantic. Would he be willing to change for me? Somehow, I doubted it. Chip was Chip, as solid and dependable as any guy could be. And about as romantic as a rock.

3

We were scheduled to leave for camp at twelve-thirty
sharp, right after church. What a joke! First of all, a
lot of kids didn't go to church that morning because
they were home packing. Then they ended up trying
to get *into* the church parking lot with all their stuff
just as hundreds of church people were trying to get
out of the parking lot to hurry home and take their
pot roasts out of the oven or whatever.

I was glad Mom and Tom had insisted we pack the
night before. We had all gone to church together as
a family, which is unusual because I'm usually the
only one who goes. But I think Mom and Tom were
concerned about us being away at camp—especially
about Max. I know Mom was praying he wouldn't
forget to take his medicine.

We were taking three slightly dilapidated school
buses to camp. I put my sleeping bag and suitcase on

a seat in the first bus. I glanced around for Nick and frowned. He was just standing there, like he was waiting for someone. I started to say something to him just as some of his friends from his fancy-schmatzy private school arrived—and they all climbed aboard the second bus! I turned and punched my sleeping bag. If he didn't want his stepsister tagging along, well, that was fine with me. I'd hang around with Max.

Max really didn't seem too happy about this trip. I knew he didn't mind leaving home or anything, but sometimes Max is a fish out of water. He's a brain, sure, but he's still only an eleven-year-old boy and I know sometimes he feels out of place with high school kids even though he tutors our entire varsity football team.

I wasn't surprised when he climbed onto my bus and sat across from me. Max and I can trust each other—he knows that I practice singing into my hairbrush in front of the mirror; I know about his secret love for Twinkies and how he likes to dress up like a scientist when he's conducting an experiment or something. He'd die if anyone else knew.

Max and I were alone on the bus with about thirty bedrolls and maybe a hundred suitcases. All the other kids had come on the bus long enough to stake out a seat, then jumped off and gone to talk with their friends. I leaned across the aisle and whispered: "Max, know what?"

He shook his head. "What?"

"I'm a little nervous."

"About what?"

"About not knowing anybody."

"You know me."

"You know what I mean."

Max nodded, and his big brown eyes seemed to glisten. "I brought a copy of *Scientific American*. If you don't have anything to do, you can read it."

"No, thanks."

"I brought Mildred. If you get bored, you can play with her."

"You brought your gerbil?" I couldn't believe it. "Where is she?"

"She's in a special can at the top of my duffel bag," Max explained. "But don't tell anybody."

"I won't. But I don't think I'll want to play with her, either."

"Tom slipped me a carton of Twinkies. If you really get lonely, you can have one. I have enough to last a week."

Twinkies were Max's comfort food, but I didn't have Max's sweet tooth. "Thanks, Max, but you keep them. Maybe you can open your own concession stand with them if you get bored."

Just then we heard someone blow a whistle. We looked out the window to see Mom and Tom standing with Doug Richlett, probably telling him to take good care of us. Then they looked in our direction and waved. Mom blew kisses and encouraged Steffie to do it, too. Embarrassing.

Kids began to swarm onto the buses. One woman ran by with a camera, screaming, "Lincoln! You forgot this!" Another lady was pulling on Doug Richlett's sleeve proclaiming that her daughter was allergic to ant stings, bee stings, and caterpillar bites. Little kids were gazing up at the buses as if they were glamorous conveyances that might someday, when they were old enough, whisk them off to a magical place called "Spring Camp."

I watched closely as the kids streamed onto the buses. Aside from Mom, Tom, and Steffie, I didn't see anyone I knew. A few of the kids from church looked familiar. But I'd always gone to church with Chip and I hadn't really gotten to know anyone well. I hugged my bundled sleeping bag close to me on the seat so nobody would sit with me and try to make me talk.

The driver started the bus and the old engine roared to life. Then he took the bus out of gear, and we lurched forward, then circled the parking lot.

The crowd kept waving as we circled, and a tall,

skinny figure ran out of the church. It was Chip—
late as usual. He ran to the entrance of the parking
lot so we'd have to pass by him on our way out.

What was he doing? He didn't know which bus I
was on, but he cupped his hands and yelled as we
went by, "Bye Cassie. Have fun!"

I sank back in my seat. How embarrassing! I
thought for a second about waving back at him, but
everyone would probably think I was absolutely
nuts. I had just enough time to look back and see
him yell at the second and third bus, too. Honestly,
sometimes that boy was certifiably loony!

Three hot and bumpy hours later, we pulled off
the interstate onto a long, dusty road. A wooden
sign proclaimed that we were on the two hundred
acres of Camp Katumba, "Home of horses, hayrides,
and happiness." I hadn't seen any one of the three
yet.

"The horses will be nice," I called across the aisle
to Max. I had to yell to be heard above the noise of
the bus, the other kids, and the wind that whistled
through our open windows. "And swimming. It will
be nice to swim in this heat."

A girl behind me giggled and tapped me on the
shoulder. "First time?" she asked.

I nodded and pulled a flyaway piece of hair out of
my mouth.

"The lake is spring-fed," the girl yelled. "The water is *freezing*."

"Freezing? Can't we swim?" I yelled back. The dust in the air was beginning to make my nose itch.

She grinned. "Sure. But the water's still freezing. Getting in is the hardest part."

The road we were on forked, and over to the right I could see a huge barn with horses tied out front. "Oh, they're beautiful," I said, noticing one particular black horse who seemed as delicate as a china figurine. "Can we ride today?"

It was quieter now that the bus had slowed, and the girl behind me nodded. "Usually they offer trail rides after lunch. Since the horses are saddled and ready to go, I'm sure somebody can ride today. We usually take turns by cabins."

We followed the road to the left and passed several large buildings. "That's the chapel," the girl behind me said, pointing to a large A-frame building with stone walls. "And that new building there is the cafeteria. Behind it is the first-aid station and a pay phone, if you need to make a call."

The bus came to a sudden, lurching stop—"May it rest in peace," Max remarked—and I looked around. We were in a clearing, surrounded by tall oak trees. Through the trees I could see small cabins arranged in two circles.

"Those are the girls' cabins over there," the girl said, pointing to the right. "They're all named after birds. The boys' cabins are animals." She grinned. "Appropriate, right?"

I laughed. I liked this girl. She had bright red hair—so bright it was almost orange—and freckles crowded her face. "What's your name?" I asked.

"Meghann Mead," she replied, tossing her hair. "I come every year. My two best friends in the world will be here this week, too, and I haven't seen them since last year. I'm so excited!"

"You mean we're not the only ones here?"

Meghann laughed. "No. There are only 150 kids from Canova Cove. A couple of other churches from other towns bring their kids here this week, too." She giggled. "I can't wait."

Well, if Meghann was any proof, Tom was right about one thing—good friends are made at camp. But Meghann wasn't going to be my friend, I knew that right away. When her two friends showed up, I probably wouldn't see her again. I turned away from her, my heart sinking.

My life was in a boring rut at home. Now, at camp, it would be in a *lonely* boring rut.

4

We hauled our stuff off the buses, checked with Doug for our cabin assignments, then trucked our suitcases and junk over to the cabins. I was in the "Bluebird" cabin with Meghann, her two unidentified friends, and two other girls who were best friends, Rachel Cooper and Emily Payne. Our counselor turned out to be Jane Richlett, Doug's wife. She slept in a little closet of a room on the other side of the bathroom and I was tempted to ask her if she wanted to trade bunks with me. I might as well sleep alone—it wasn't like I had any friends to bunk with.

After we settled in and made our beds (if you can call throwing a sleeping bag over a plastic mattress "making a bed"), Jane gave us our camp notebooks. I glanced over the week's schedule and gloomily noticed that there were huge blocks of free time to be bored in. Doug scheduled meetings in the morning and after dinner each night, a cabin cleanup time every morning, and each night there was a different activity after the evening meeting. Aside from that, we were free to do whatever we wanted.

The schedule said that at five o'clock we were supposed to go to the chapel, so I met Max outside and we slipped in with the crowd of campers walking along the dirt road. Our group was noticeably larger than it had been at our church this morning.

Inside the A-frame chapel, I looked for Meghann's red hair and spotted her down front, with her arms linked through the arms of two blonde girls I'd never seen before. I sighed. Why couldn't I have a friend here? Why hadn't I asked Andrea to come?

Doug climbed the stairs to the platform and held up his hand for quiet. "Hi," he said, smiling at the group, "I'm Doug Richlett and I'll be acting as head honcho this week for all you guys, so everybody just listen up."

I could sense that everyone was restless—it was dinnertime, and we were all ready to eat. "We're going to have a great time at camp this week," Doug went on. "There are only four rules I want you to obey."

A collective groan rose from the crowd. "Number one is no Marlboros," Doug said, grinning. "We don't want to start any forest fires, so we counselors don't want to see anyone smoking. So what's rule number one?"

"No Marlboros," we all mumbled.

Max leaned over and whispered, "Shucks, I forgot my Camels."

"Shut up, Max. Be serious." But the ridiculous thought of Max with a cigarette hanging out of his mouth did make me smile.

"Rule number two," Doug continued, "is no messin'. No messing around in the lake without a lifeguard, no messing around after lights out, and no messing around with private property. Everybody got that?"

"No messin'," we all chanted.

"Good." Doug nodded. "Rule number three is simple. No makin' out. Does anybody need me to explain that one?"

Several girls giggled and the boys rolled their eyes. One smart-aleck guy down front stood up and threw his hands in the air: "Uh, gee, Doug, what do you mean by that?"

"Sit down," Doug said good-naturedly. "I'll explain it to you later."

The mouthy guy sat down, and I was surprised to see that he was sitting with Nick. Who was this kid, and how did Nick know him? Maybe they were in the same cabin.

"Rule number four is no matches," Doug said. "We've had a dry spring and the forest ranger has warned us that the woods are dry. In fact, we will have a fire drill at some point during this camp. When you hear the fire alarm sound, go quickly to the lake and stand at the edge, no matter what time of day or night it is. Understand?"

We all nodded. "Good. There's just one more thing before we eat dinner," Doug said, reaching into his briefcase. He pulled out a wide gold fabric belt with a large shiny belt buckle. "This is the Golden Belt of Katumba. Blessed is the camper who wears the Golden Belt of Katumba, for at the end of the week, he shall receive glory and honor and a prize for himself and his cabin."

A couple of kids snickered, but Doug went on. "We are having competition between the cabins, and these contests will last all week. But the most important contest of all will involve the Golden Belt of Katumba. I know a riddle. The camper who can answer my riddle will wear the Golden Belt of Katumba. Anyone who then tells him or her the answer to the riddle will be given the Golden Belt of Katumba, and whoever is wearing the blessed belt at week's end will win a special after-hours party for all who are in the cabin."

"I could answer a riddle," Max whispered. "Riddles are easy if you just think logically."

"It won't be fair if you win it," I shot back. "Geniuses aren't allowed to play."

Max just grinned, but I didn't think going after a golden belt was his style. He was probably counting the minutes until he could take Mildred the gerbil out in the woods for some science experiment, then I'd be left really and truly alone.

"Think on this, O campers," Doug recited. "My riddle is this: What walks on four legs in the morning, on two legs in the afternoon, and on three legs at night?"

You could almost hear brains clicking, but the spell was broken when Doug smiled and said: "Think on it, but the last one to the dining hall has to clean up!"

The food at dinner was OK. It might even have tasted good if there'd been someone for me to talk with. But I sat at a table surrounded by strangers who talked to each other and didn't even seem to notice me. After dinner, I walked across the field between the cafeteria and the camp office to the pay phone. There was a big sign over the phone that said For Emergencies Only, but I figured this was nearly an emergency. I dialed home.

"Harris residence," a gruff voice answered.

"Uncle Jacob! Why aren't you in the Bahamas?"

"I leave first thing in the morning," he barked back. "Cassie? Is everything all right?"

"We're all fine," I said, turning to watch a squirrel chase his tail. "It's really nice here, Uncle Jacob. You'd like it."

"So why are you calling? Don't tell me you've run out of spending money already!"

"No, I just thought I'd let you guys know we made it here OK."

"That's nice." Uncle Jacob was quiet, and I knew he was probably wishing I was sitting in front of him at the kitchen counter. He wasn't used to counseling me long-distance.

"Do you want to speak to your mom?"

"No, that's OK. I don't want to bother her vacation. Just tell her we're OK, please?"

"I will. Want to speak to Tom?"

"No, don't bother him, either."

Uncle Jacob's voice softened. "Are you having a good time?"

I bit my lip. Something in me wanted to yell, "No! I don't know anybody, and I walk everywhere by myself when everyone else is with at least one friend." But I didn't. Instead, I swallowed hard and said, "Sure. Max is going to try to win the Golden Belt of Katumba."

Uncle Jacob chuckled. "Sounds like fun. Well, honey, if you're all right, I'll be sure to tell your mom and Tom."

"Thanks, Uncle Jake. Have a nice cruise, OK?"

"I will."

"Bring me back a souvenir?"

"If you'll bring me one."

"OK. I promise."

I hung up the phone and walked back to my cabin with my head down. A souvenir? I never wanted to see anything again that would remind me of this place.

5

Doug Richlett looked a little tired at breakfast on Monday morning. But I didn't have any trouble sleeping that first night. What else was I going to do? There wasn't anyone to talk to . . . not for me, anyway.

Meghann, on the other hand, never stopped talking. Her two best friends turned out to be twins, Sondra and Signe Weaver from Melbourne. The three of them spent all night whispering under a blanket. Rachel and Emily, who were on the bunk across from me, got mad at each other and sulked in silence until they went to sleep. Jane Richlett knocked on our door at six-thirty in the morning and congratulated us on being so quiet after lights out. I didn't want to tell her I was quiet because I was miserable.

That morning it was hard for all six of us to get

into the bathroom to do our hair, so we were nearly too late for breakfast. But I managed to get in line and grab a box of Rice Krispies and a carton of milk. Best of all, Max was sitting at a table with just one other kid. At least I'd have someone to talk to.

"Hi," I said, sliding my tray next to Max's. I sat down and prayed quickly over my food: "Lord, bless this food and *please* help me get through the day."

Max was testing a suspicious helping of grits with his spoon. "Isn't it amazing?" he asked. "They turn to rubber as they cool. Look, Cassie, I could peel these grits off my plate like one of those rubber pools of fake vomit."

"Be quiet, Max." I smiled at the boy sitting on the other side of Max. He kept his head down, staring intently at his food. As I looked at him, I wasn't surprised he was hanging around with Max. This boy had to be at least in seventh grade, or he wouldn't be here at camp, but he was really short. He was no taller than Max, and Max was only eleven. "I'm Max's sister, Cassie," I said, trying to get him to look up.

The boy slowly looked up and turned his face toward me. "Hi," he said simply. "I'm Lincoln Meyers."

I gasped. A spot right above his eye looked like a green and purple egg. "What happened to you?" I asked. "Did you fall out of your bunk?"

Lincoln lowered his head, embarrassed, but Max spoke up. "See that guy over there wiping tables?"

I looked across the room and saw the dark-haired boy from last night, the smart aleck who had been sitting with Nick. "Yeah, I see him. Who's he?"

"He's Ethan Wilcox," Max said. "He goes to school with Nick and they're in the same cabin."

"So? What does that have to do with Lincoln's bruise?"

Max gave me his just-be-patient look. "Last night after lights out, Ethan organized a pillow fight."

"So?" I raised an eyebrow.

"So all the guys' cabins got involved and Ethan's cabin was getting beat."

"So?"

"So Ethan decided to make the odds more even."

"How, Max?" Honestly, he could take *forever* to tell a story.

Lincoln raised his head. "He put a rock in his pillowcase," he blurted out. "He creamed me on the side of the head."

"Lincoln nearly lost consciousness," Max added. "It was very dramatic. Doug Richlett came running out in his nightshirt and everyone got in trouble."

"Is that why Ethan's wiping tables?"

Both boys nodded. "He's got to wipe down all the tables today," Lincoln said. "And if he does one more thing to break the rules, Doug said Ethan would be sent home."

"Really?" I didn't know Doug would actually send anybody home.

Max nodded. "Yeah. Doug will call his parents and they'll have to drive all the way up here and get him."

"Sounds good to me," I said, watching Ethan wipe tables. I knew guys were rough, but putting a rock into a pillowcase seemed a little too rough even for a big guy like Ethan. As he wiped tables, though, he didn't seem the least bit upset over his punishment. He acted like it was really a cool thing to do, and he kept going over to girls' tables and leaning down to talk.

Doug Richlett walked to the cafeteria's public address system and tapped on the microphone to get our attention. "Attention, Katumba campers," he said, his voice a little raspy. "Good morning. After breakfast is cabin cleanup. You must go back to your cabin and get it ready for inspection. The cleanest cabin will eat first today at lunch, and the cabin who wins the dirty sock award will have cleanup duty." He looked over at Ethan. "With Ethan Wilcox, that is."

Ethan held out his hands and bowed, and a group of girls at a nearby table giggled. What a jerk the guy was. All anyone had to do was look at Lincoln Meyer's face and they'd see what a total loser this Ethan Wilcox was.

I didn't realize I was staring at him until he looked up and saw me. I looked away quickly, but I could feel my face burning. I tried to think of something to talk about so Ethan would think I was deep in conversation.

"So Doug Richlett wears a nightshirt?" I casually asked Max.

Max raised an eyebrow. "Yeah. A Pittsburgh Steelers shirt."

Lincoln grinned. "Why anyone would wear something like that is beyond me."

"Actually, statistically, they should be better next season than they were last year," Max said. "They've got that new quarterback, you know, and—"

"So, it's the egghead and the egg face." The voice came from right behind me, and I knew who it had to be, but I didn't want to look up. Neither did Lincoln Meyers. He flushed and looked down at his plate.

But Max glared up at Ethan Wilcox. "Only people with little minds resort to name-calling," he said, throwing his puny chest out a little. I had to admire his spunk.

"Who's this, Maxwell Smart?" the voice went on. "Did you bribe this girl to sit with you?"

I clenched my eyes tightly, not wanting to even see him. What a jerk! He reminded me of Andrea's boyfriend, who was always picking on kids in our school.

Max could stand up to him, though. "This is my sister, Ethan, and I don't have to bribe her to sit with me. She knows class when she sees it."

"Oh yeah?" Ethan squatted on the floor next to me. There was no way I could avoid looking at him; he practically thrust his face into mine. I had never seen him this close. He had dark, snapping eyes and a square jaw. He smiled at me in a confident way that made me feel angry and embarrassed at the same time.

"Your sister, huh? Do you have a name, pretty lady?"

I could have thrown my soggy Rice Krispies over his head with pleasure, but I tried to stay calm. "It's Cassiopeia Priscilla Perkins," I said, rudely pushing my chair back. "My friends call me Cassie. But anyone who would do this," I said, pointing to Lincoln's purpling bruise, "is not my friend." I picked up my tray and stood up. "I'd love to continue this wonderful conversation, but I've got to go help my friends clean the cabin."

There! I walked away with my head high. What a total creep! Now if I could just figure out why my hands were trembling and my cheeks were burning.

6

I thought I'd be the invisible roommate back at the cabin, but when the other girls came in, I was an instant celebrity.

"We saw Ethan Wilcox at your table," Meghann said, falling across my bunk. "What did he say? Do you know how lucky you are? He's just the best looking guy at this camp!"

"She's checked them all out, too," Sondra added. "After breakfast Meghann walked all around and rated every guy here."

"Ethan got a ten plus," Signe said, lying down on her bunk. "He should be a model or something. He is so fine!"

Rachel and Emily agreed, so I guessed they weren't fighting anymore. "He goes to our school," Rachel said. "And there's not a girl at Princeton who wouldn't give her right arm to go out with him. He's the hottest thing on campus."

"Really?" I asked, plopping down on my bunk. "I think he's a jerk."

"Well, if you don't want him, there are plenty of girls who do!" Emily said, winking at Rachel.

"Doesn't he have a girlfriend?" Meghann asked, sitting up straighter. She clapped her hands and her eyes gleamed. "Or is he available?"

Rachel sighed. "He's available, all right. Sure, he goes with all the girls, but with no one in particular."

"We ought to ask someone in his cabin if he likes redheads," Signe said, looking at Meghann, "or blondes."

I sighed. What a boring conversation. "My brother's in his cabin," I said. "You can ask him."

Emily crinkled her nose. "Your brother? That little dweeb you ate with at breakfast?"

"My other brother," I explained. "Nick Harris."

"Nick Harris is your brother?" Rachel and Emily exclaimed together.

"He's really fine, too," Sondra added.

"Super-fine," echoed Signe.

I nodded. "He's my stepbrother."

I could tell from their faces that suddenly they saw me in a different light. Last night all of them had ignored me, but now I had at least two things going for me—I was Nick's sister and Ethan Wilcox had stopped by my table at breakfast.

"This is great!" Meghann said, her freckles glowing. "Cassie, you can introduce me to Ethan, and Sondra can have Nick, and Signe can have the little dweeb!"

They all burst into laughter as if she were the wittiest person in the world, but I was beginning to dislike all of them. "Max isn't a dweeb," I said, trying to stay calm. "He's a genius. He's in the tenth grade at Astronaut High and he's only eleven years old. He knows more than all of you put together."

Emily smirked. "So? Sorry, Cassie, if we hurt your feelings, but you have to admit you looked a little weird sitting there with those two little guys."

I couldn't take any more. They could clean this cabin by themselves. "Oh yeah? Well, sitting with those two little guys got Ethan Wilcox's attention, didn't it?"

I walked out and let the door slam.

I walked around the camp for a little while just to kill time before the morning meeting. Camp Katumba was in a really pretty spot. Wild peacocks roamed all over the place and I nearly got close enough to touch one of them, but at the last minute something spooked him and he ran away.

The lake was as cold as ice water. Standing on the

diving platform, I could see straight to the bottom, where it was littered with algae-covered stones.

The other kids were beginning to hike up the road from the cabins to the chapel, so I got up and took a shortcut through a field. Up ahead, two girls were walking with a guy in between them. I couldn't hear them, but I could tell he was teasing them. At one point he put his arms around their waists, and they backed away as if he were tickling them.

At that point it wasn't hard to guess who the guy was. I took bigger steps and caught up with them. Sure enough, it was Ethan Wilcox. I passed them in a huff, not even glancing in their direction, but I was surprised that I felt a little flicker of jealousy. Why had he stopped by my table this morning? Did he really think I was pretty? If he did, why was he messing around with those girls?

Ethan saw me. "Hey, Lassie," he called, but I only walked faster and didn't turn around. My eyes filled with tears, though. Was he calling me "Lassie" because he thought I was a dog? That's what he meant, I knew. And I still thought he was the lowest, the meanest, the most vile human being on the face of the earth, no matter how good-looking he was.

I sat with Max and Lincoln at lunch and again at dinner, not because I wanted Ethan Wilcox to come over, but because I didn't think anyone else would want me around. I would have sat with Nick, but Nick was often with Ethan, and I wasn't going within a foot of that particular species of manhood.

Lincoln and Max were hatching a plan to win the Golden Belt of Katumba. No one had answered Doug's riddle correctly. Max said he knew the answer, but he wouldn't tell what it was. Lincoln was trying to convince him to win the belt for their cabin.

"Don't you want a party on the last night of camp?" he asked Max. "Just think—of all these guys at camp, we can be the ones to get the party, Max. They'll all just die if we pull it off."

"Why don't you just tell Lincoln the answer and let him win it?" I suggested.

Max sighed and looked at me. "That wouldn't be fair, Cassie. You said it wouldn't be fair if I answered the riddle."

I glanced over to the table where Nick and Ethan and their friends were making a loud ruckus. "I've changed my mind," I said simply. "I think it would be great if you *younger* guys won the belt. It would teach all those other guys a lesson."

". . . that might doesn't make right," Max said thoughtfully. "OK, I'll do it. I could answer the riddle before tonight's meeting."

Lincoln clapped his hands. "Great! And in the meantime, I'm sure I can think of the answer, and I can win it back from anyone who might take it from you. And we could help the other guys in our cabin—not by telling them, but just by helping them—so we could win it back and make sure it stays in our cabin. That way we'll win the party for sure!"

"It could work." Max nodded thoughtfully. "If we're lucky."

Doug gave Max the Golden Belt of Katumba in front of the entire group. I felt a little embarrassed for him because Doug made a big deal out of it, but it was all in fun. Besides, no one else had been able to figure out Doug's riddle.

"What goes on four legs in the morning, two legs at noon, and three legs at night?" Doug asked.

Max leaned forward and whispered in Doug's ear. Doug nodded and whipped out the Golden Belt of Katumba with a flourish. "Wear it well, my wise friend," he said, fastening it around Max's slender waist. "And give it freely to anyone else who gives you the correct answer."

The five other guys in Max's cabin whooped in delight, and I looked over and saw that Ethan and his group watched with interest. They acted like the

whole thing was silly, but they'd probably do anything to win a free party on the last night of camp. I
reminded myself to tell Max to watch his step. Somewhere out there in the night could be a rock-laden
pillowcase with his name on it.

The evening service was interesting. Doug spoke
on how we could know the Bible was the Word of
God, but I spent most of the time wondering how a
crud like Ethan Wilcox could end up in a church
camp. His parents—no, his *zookeepers*—probably
wanted a week off and sent him away. A church
camp probably sounded like a nice, safe place.

After the service Doug told us we were going to
play capture the flag. "Each team will have a flag,"
Doug explained. "The girls' flag will be located at
the southernmost point of camp, and the boys' flag
will be at the north end of camp. Each of you will
wear an arm band around your upper arm, too."

He held up a piece of bright orange tape, which
he had Jane tie around his arm. "If someone on the
enemy team pulls the arm band off your arm, you're
out of the game," he said. "Go back to your cabin
and wait. But as long as you're in the game, the
object is to advance to the enemies' flag and capture
it. The team who successfully defends their own flag
and captures the enemy's flag is the victor."

A murmur of excitement rose from the group. "It

will be dark out there," Doug warned us, "so carry a flashlight and be careful. You have twenty minutes to go to your cabins and put on grubby clothes—"

"—and mosquito repellent," Jane interrupted.

"Right," Doug said. "Meet back here in twenty minutes."

My cabinmates were all excited. "I know whose arm band I'm going to get," Meghann bubbled. "Ethan Wilcox's. I'll bring it back here tonight and sleep with it under my pillow."

"You're crazy," Rachel said. "He wouldn't let you within ten feet of him. He runs track, you know. You couldn't catch him."

"I'm going to try, too," Signe said.

"Aren't you all missing the point?" I asked, pulling a black sweatshirt over my head. "We're supposed to go after the boys' flag, not just Ethan's arm band. It will have to be a team effort."

Meghann sniffed. "Honestly, Cassie, you take the fun out of everything."

I squirted my clothes with bug spray, grabbed my flashlight, and left the cabin. I'd show them. I'd get Ethan's arm band, and I wouldn't even break a sweat doing it. Plus, I'd help the girls capture the guys' flag.

I stayed in the shadows for about five minutes after the game started. I could hear whoops and screams and laughter, but I couldn't see anyone within twenty feet of where I was. Time to put my plan into action.

If I knew Ethan and Nick, and I was sure I did, they'd be playing it cool, not running around in the dark like madmen. All I had to do was find where they were sitting the game out.

It didn't take me long. I walked calmly along the road, under the streetlight, like I wasn't even playing the game and didn't have a care in the world. Outside the snack shop, by the picnic tables, there were two shadowy figures. I could smell cigarette smoke.

"Someone's coming! Put that out!"

"It's OK, Nick, it's only me," I said, walking calmly over to the guys. Ethan was stepping on a cigarette; Nick looked embarrassed. Both of them, I noticed, were wearing their glow-in-the-dark arm bands.

"Who's that?" Ethan asked Nick.

"Nobody," Nick answered. "Just my sister."

Ethan looked more closely at me. "You're the brain's sister. Cassio-something."

"You're brilliant," I answered. I climbed up on top of the picnic table and tried to act bored. "What are you guys doing here when you're supposed to be out chasing some dumb flag?"

"We could ask you the same question," Ethan said, smiling at me in his cocky way. He sat down next to me on the table; I could have reached out and ripped off his arm band easily. *Patience,* I told myself. *Make sure you can get away.*

"What do you want?" Nick asked impatiently.

I shrugged. "Nothing. I'm just bored. I think this game is dumb."

Ethan tilted his head and laughed in surprise. "Really? What would you like to do?"

"Oh, I don't know. Maybe ride a horse or go swimming or go to town . . ." I rattled off a list of things I didn't care a thing about doing. Somehow I had to get Ethan off balance so I could rip the band off his arm without his being able to grab me. I had one idea.

"Ouch!" I slapped the back of my hand.

"What happened?" Ethan asked.

"A bug bit me. I think it crawled under the table." I jumped down to the ground and peered under the table. "Come on, you guys, help me find it. What if it was a black widow spider or something?"

"Cassie, we're not going to find anything in the dark," Nick grumbled, but he stooped down to look under the table, too. Finally Ethan moved over and stuck his head under the table ledge.

While he was off-balance, I snatched the band from his arm, my fingers brushing against his denim jacket. I gave a good, strong tug and the thin plastic

56

snapped. "Hey!" Ethan yelled, but it was too late. I was off and running.

I don't think he even tried to follow me, so after a few minutes I slowed down and slid into the shadow of a tree to catch my breath. I put the arm band into my pocket and laughed quietly. I didn't care who won the stupid flag game. All that mattered was that I had Ethan Wilcox's arm band in my pocket.

7

I went back to the cabin. I felt absolutely wiped out from all that running, but I couldn't wait to show the other girls what I had. They were taking their time, though, so I took advantage of the empty cabin to brush my teeth and take a quick shower. I was ready for bed before long, and they still hadn't come in.

I lay down on my sleeping bag and finally heard their voices from the open window. "Rachel, it was your fault," Emily whined. "If you hadn't let go of the flagpole, they never would have been able to carry it off."

"I couldn't hold on to it forever!" Rachel defended herself. "How could I? With those big guys like Ethan all over the place, how was I supposed to hold on? At least I didn't lose my arm band like Meghann and her friends."

"I couldn't help it," Meghann said as they all came into the cabin. "Ethan Wilcox jumped out at me from behind. I couldn't help it."

"That's impossible," I said flatly. They all looked at me as if the bed itself had decided to speak.

"How do you know it's impossible?" Meghann demanded. "You weren't even there. Miss Team Effort didn't even help at all."

"Yes I did." I sat up and reached for the orange arm band in my jeans pocket.

"What's that?" Signe asked. "Did you beat up your little brother and take his arm band?"

"No. I took it from Ethan Wilcox."

All five of them looked at me for a minute, then burst into laughter. "You're crazy," Sondra said finally. "Ethan was in on the game there at the end, and he was wearing an arm band. He took about twenty of ours, though, and the boys won."

"That's not right. He shouldn't have been playing because I took his arm band at the beginning of the game," I said. "He must have taken someone else's."

Meghann shook her head. "It was a good try, Cassie, but no one's going to believe that story."

"You can ask my brother Nick!"

Emily laughed. "Nick wasn't even around."

I sat in confusion and thought. Could Nick have given Ethan his arm band? Or did Ethan take an extra arm band from someone like Max or Lincoln?

I lay down on my bunk and turned my back to the other girls. Let them say I was a liar. I knew the truth, and it was only one more thing to prove to me that Ethan Wilcox was scum. He had broken every rule at camp, except maybe the one about makin' out, and he didn't deserve to be here. Why on earth had he come?

The other girls kept arguing and complaining even after lights out. I picked up Ethan's arm band from the floor and tucked it under my pillow. If they didn't believe it was his, then they didn't deserve to see it.

At breakfast on Tuesday morning, Max and Lincoln were all smiles. Max was wearing the Golden Belt of Katumba and frankly enjoying the privileges it brought. He hadn't had to walk from the cabins to the cafeteria, Doug had given him a ride on an ATV. He was served breakfast immediately without standing in line.

"That's not all," Lincoln told me as we ate eggs and bacon, "but last night during the game a tree branch broke loose and fell right in front of Max. If Max had been standing ten inches over, he'd have been hit."

"Wow." I looked over at Max. "What a lucky break."

Max shook his head. "Luck had nothing to do with it. It is a coincidence that I was in the area at all."

"No! That belt is good luck," Lincoln went on earnestly. "Just look at how everything's going right for Max. I wish—" He swallowed and stirred his eggs. "Well, I could use some good luck. Things don't always go so well for me."

"About last night," I interrupted. "Did anything unusual happen last night?"

"Max had the incredible good luck of pulling five girls' arm bands," Lincoln said. "He figured out a way to snip them off with fingernail clippers when the girls weren't looking."

"You didn't lose your own arm bands?" I asked.

Max made a face. "Honestly, Cass, do you think anyone could take it from me?"

"Don't get too high and mighty there, Mr. Golden Belt," I reminded him. "Someone like Ethan Wilcox could come along and knock you back down to earth."

Max grinned at me and Lincoln rambled on: "I doubt it. It's incredible, the good luck that belt has brought Max. Why, just this morning Max stepped outside and found forty-five cents in the sand! Can you believe that? It just doesn't happen to everyone . . ."

But I wasn't listening anymore. I got out of my chair and walked over to the table where Nick and Ethan Wilcox were sitting.

"Why did you cheat last night?" I demanded. I looked Ethan straight in the eye. I wasn't blushing now. All my roommates thought I was a liar, thanks to his cheating, and the spark of indignation had flared within me.

"Well, good morning to you, too," Ethan said, smiling at me. "How'd you do last night? How many other guys did you manage to rip off?"

"I didn't rip anyone off," I answered. "I was just playing the game."

"Come on, Cassie, forget it," Nick urged. "Go on back and talk to Max."

Ethan and I both ignored him. "Well, I wasn't playing the game until you pulled that little stunt," Ethan said. He lowered his voice and I had to bend closer to hear him. "So after you made the game look like so much fun, I borrowed Nick's little arm band and joined in the game."

He tilted his head and leaned closer to me. "But I was looking for you, sweetie, and I couldn't find you anywhere." There was something in his tone that was a little dangerous, a little teasing, and I suddenly felt uncomfortable. I pulled away.

"That wasn't fair," I said simply. "You were out of the game. You weren't supposed to be playing."

"I wasn't even in the game until after I met you," Ethan replied, aware that other kids were listening. He smiled and took my hand. "Doesn't that sound romantic?"

I jerked my hand away from his warm grasp and spun around so quickly that I bumped into a poor kid who was carrying about five trays loaded with breakfast dishes. The kid went down, the dishes flew everywhere, and the front of my shirt was soaked with orange juice and bits of egg. While everyone looked and laughed, I ran out of the cafeteria.

While I changed my clothes, the other girls came back for cabin cleanup. Fortunately, no one said a thing about my accident in the cafeteria. I would have either burst into tears or smacked anyone who mentioned it. None of it would have happened if not for Ethan Wilcox.

In the morning chapel service, I sat with Max and Lincoln but couldn't stop myself from looking over to where Ethan and Nick sat. I was so mad I was tempted to call home and tell Mom and Tom to come pick me up. While they were at it, they could send a pit bull or something that would teach Ethan Wilcox some manners. I'd be happy to sic a dog on him.

I don't know why, but Ethan kept looking over in my direction, too. More than once I caught him looking my way, and when I caught his eye, he smiled that cocky smile of his that made me boiling mad. After a while it became a game: I'd look, he'd look, he'd smile, I'd look away. Then I'd look back and glare at him.

By the end of the hour, though, the pattern had changed. I'd look, he'd look, he'd smile, I'd glare, he'd look hurt, I'd stop glaring, he'd smile, and I'd smile back. I don't know why I stopped hating him, but somehow, I did. When he gave me that hurt look, his cheating on the game last night didn't seem like such a big deal. After all, was it really so terrible that he tried to hold my hand in the cafeteria? And it was my fault I bumped into the kid with the dishes—Ethan didn't push me or anything.

I tuned back into Doug's lesson just in time to hear him say that we should forgive people who upset us. *OK, Lord*, I prayed, *I forgive Ethan Wilcox for being such a creep*. There. Now if I could just get through the rest of the week.

We had free time after lunch and it wasn't our
cabin's turn to ride horses. I didn't want to swim, so
I dug a book out of my suitcase and took it outside.
Maybe I could find a nice tree and read a while.

There was a nature trail behind the cabins, so I
tucked my book in my back pocket and walked
along the trail for a while. Sometimes I like being
alone. I like to write poetry and I enjoy singing, and
it's easier to do both of those things when you're
alone.

Come to think of it, I honestly didn't know why
I felt so lonely at camp. Maybe it was because everyone else seemed to be with friends. Or maybe I was
disappointed that Chip hadn't come. Maybe I was
just upset with my cabinmates. Whatever it was, I

knew if something didn't change, I'd be miserable the rest of the week.

I found a big rock under a tree just off the path, so I stepped carefully through the thick ferns that surrounded it, watching for snakes. "Make plenty of noise," Max told me once. "They're more afraid of you than you are of them." Sure.

I settled on the rock and opened my book, when suddenly I smelled smoke. I looked up and sniffed the air. Was there a forest fire? Should I run? Tell the others? What should I do?

Then I saw the source of the smoke. Ethan Wilcox. He was on the trail, alone, and he was smoking. He didn't see me, he was just walking quietly along, with one hand in his pocket and the other holding his cigarette. His eyes were on the ground, as if he were thinking hard about something.

"You know, you really shouldn't smoke," I called. "It'll kill you and give you bad breath, too."

He looked at me and I thought he was startled, but he took another drag and blew smoke out his nose. Disgusting, actually. Then he put the cigarette down on the ground and carefully ground it out with his shoe. "You're right," he said finally. "I don't know why I do it."

"Max says nicotine is the most addictive drug in

this country," I told him. "So I don't know why you ever started."

Ethan stood there with his hands in his pockets and looked at me. Standing there alone, in his white cotton shirt and jeans, with his dark hair and eyes, he *was* gorgeous. No doubt about it.

"Is that all you ever do?" he asked. "Go around preaching at people?"

I felt my cheeks begin to flush. "I'm not preaching," I said simply. "Just telling you the facts."

"Oh." He looked over at my rock. "Can I join you?"

"Here?" I couldn't believe it. "Uh, you can have the whole rock. I was just getting ready to go down to the lake."

"Are you going swimming?"

"Uh, maybe." Swimming was the last thing in the world I had planned to do, but I didn't want Ethan to think I was following him around camp. Whatever he did, I'd do something else.

"Maybe I'll see you there."

He walked off, on down the trail, and I watched him go until I couldn't see his white shirt through the trees. He was such a mystery. I didn't understand him at all. But I held one comforting thought: something I said made him put his cigarette out. Maybe there was hope for Ethan Wilcox yet.

I didn't want to, but I put on my bathing suit and looked in the tiny cabin mirror to make sure I looked OK. You never know—sometimes you can put on last year's bathing suit and find that you're just not the same as you were last year. My suit was black, which matched my dark hair, and there were rows of ruffles over my chest. Last year those ruffles just sort of lay across my chest. But this year they made me look, well, fluffy. I was a little self-conscious, so I grabbed a towel and draped it over my shoulders to walk down to the lake.

I brought my book along, too. I could always sit on my towel and read and say I was getting some sun, because I really had no intention of getting into that freezing water. I hate cold water. At home I always beg Uncle Jacob to keep our pool heater set high enough so the water's about the temperature of bath water, but Tom says that's wasteful and defeats the purpose of a pool. "If you want a bath, take a bath," he says. "A pool is supposed to be refreshing."

I stuck my foot into the water. Zowie! This water wasn't refreshing—it would positively send me into shock. I couldn't do it. No matter what, I couldn't get into that freezing water.

"Hey, Cassie! Watch!" I looked around and saw Meghann waving at me. She was on the diving platform, about to bounce onto the "blob," a long rubber wormlike pillow that floated on the surface of the lake. It was huge. One person sat on the far end of the blob, and when another person jumped onto the other end, the resulting punch of air shot the first person out into the water.

Signe was out on the end of the blob and Meghann was preparing to jump. Signe probably weighed 90 pounds, and Meghann was at least 130, so I held my breath and waited. Meghann jumped, and Signe squealed as she was ejected up through the air and out into the water. Up on the diving deck, Sondra cheered and clapped. "Now you go to the end, Meghann," Sondra called. "And I'll launch you."

It looked like fun, but there was still no way I was going to get wet. I spread out my towel and lay down on my stomach to read. The heroine and her friends were just about to solve the mystery when I felt something gently moving across my back. It was a twig, or a piece of moss, or a spider—I was about to yell, thinking Max was up to some trick, but it was Ethan Wilcox standing there with a long peacock feather in his hand. Behind him, wearing an expression of extreme boredom, was Nick.

"Come on in the water, Cassie," Ethan said, dropping his towel and sunglasses on my towel. "I'll send you off the blob."

"Cassie doesn't like cold water," Nick said, taking off his watch. "So you'll hold this for me, won't you, Cass?"

I was about to nod and take the watch, but Ethan grabbed my outstretched arm and pulled me to my feet. "Nonsense. You get used to the cold and then it feels good. Come on, Cass."

I left my book and towel on the ground and stupidly followed him. Ethan dropped my hand but kept walking, as confident as ever, and I had to walk fast to keep up. Nick followed behind me, and I don't think he was pleased about me tagging along.

"OK, Cassie, you go first," Ethan said. "Just jump onto the blob here at this end. Try to land in the middle or you'll slide off into the water."

I was petrified. That weird striped blob floated in the water and didn't look at all inviting. Some girl in braids waited down at the other end, and I think she was disappointed that someone bigger wasn't going to launch her into the water. I was too small to send her very far.

"Jump, Cass!"

I didn't have time to think. I jumped and landed squarely on my feet, and fell forward onto the blob. It was mushy and hot from the sun, and it was hard to get a firm footing.

"Scoot to the other end and get ready!"

I turned over and crab-crawled to the far end. I prayed that I'd go straight up in the air, so I could enter the water feet first instead of in a belly flop. I looked over at the diving deck where Ethan was preparing for a running start.

Oh no! He ran, flew through the air, and jumped with both feet firmly onto the blob. I was shot into the air, and I flew up, up, and up, and then fell, feet first, into water so cold it seemed to pull the breath right out of me.

I surfaced with my teeth chattering and swam to the edge of a floating dock with a ladder. Shivering, I waited until Nick launched Ethan into the water. He dove in head first, then came up, whooping with delight. "All right!" he yelled, but instead of coming my way, he swam away from me and climbed out onto the bank. Nick was launched then, and he hollered and joined Ethan back on the diving dock. They were going to do it again. They had both forgotten about me.

Good riddance.

I made sure I was gone by the time they came out of the water for good, and I made a determined effort not to even look at Ethan Wilcox for the rest of the day. No visits to his table at dinner. No glances in his direction during the evening service. I didn't even listen to the gossip about him that came from the girls in my cabin.

But that night, during the lip-sync contest, I found myself absolutely fascinated by him. He and the guys in his cabin—the "Raccoon" cabin—performed "California Girls" by the Beach Boys, and they were absolutely darling! At the end of the song, they stopped and said, "California girls are OK, but we like Florida girls better."

Every girl in the audience screamed. Meghann stood up and pretended to faint, and Sondra and Signe fanned her furiously. All the guys in the Raccoon cabin were good, including Nick, but Ethan was absolutely wonderful. There was just something in his attitude that made all the other guys seem kind of ordinary.

After Doug announced that the Raccoons had won, we all walked back to our cabins. I was surrounded by the happy chatter of a hundred girls, but for once, I didn't feel lonely or left out. I had a happy secret of my own: when the Raccoons told the audience they liked Florida girls better, Ethan Wilcox had been looking right at me.

9

I got up early Wednesday morning and dressed quickly. It didn't matter that Meghann, Signe, Sondra, Rachel, and Emily didn't want to walk to breakfast with me. I wanted to walk by myself. If I walked by myself, slowly, there was no telling who might join me.

I left our cabin quietly while the other girls were scrambling for hair dryers and fussing about the wet towels they left outside on the clotheslines last night. The road to the cafeteria was nearly deserted, but a few boys were straggling out of their circle of cabins and heading down to breakfast. I knew the guys would be out early. They don't have to do as much to get dressed and they all like to eat.

I found a nice tree stump to sit on by the side of the road. Anyone who came from the boys' or girls' cabins would have to pass by me, and I could just sit there until someone interesting came along. I heard footsteps and pretended to study an anthill on the ground.

"Cassie! You'll never believe it!"

Ugh. I wasn't really expecting Lincoln and Max.

"I'll never believe what?" I looked up and sighed. Could I get rid of these two before Ethan came along?

"A girl from the Cardinal cabin came up and took the belt from Max last night," Lincoln said. "She guessed the riddle."

"Who?" I asked, curious in spite of myself.

"Sarah Swan," Max said. "She's pretty smart."

"Anyway, I figured out the riddle and won it back for our cabin," Lincoln said, pointing to his waist. "Look!"

Sure enough, Lincoln Meyers was wearing the Golden Belt of Katumba. "Did you help him, Max?" I asked. "Did you give him the answer?"

"Honest, Cass, I didn't," Max said. He held up his right hand and then crossed his heart. "I only helped him think logically. I could help you, too."

Lincoln's sudden look of despair made me laugh. "That's OK, guys," I said. "You can keep the Golden Belt of Katumba. It doesn't match any of my clothes."

"That's a trivial consideration," Max said, shaking his head.

"But this is neat!" Lincoln said, glowing with excitement. "I lost my alarm clock, and after I won the belt from Max I found it. Isn't that great? It really brings good luck."

I shook my head. "I don't think so, Lincoln." I looked at Max. "Haven't you explained to him that there's no such thing as good luck?"

Max shrugged. "I've tried."

"That's not all." Lincoln's eyes grew large and he motioned for us to lean closer. He whispered: "This morning I was brushing my teeth and our counselor stuck his head in the room. It was the weirdest thing—*I knew what he was going to say! I had a feeling I had been there before!*"

I snorted. "Lincoln, that's déjà vu. Everyone has it. It has nothing to do with that belt."

Max nodded. "The going theory behind déjà vu is that it comes mostly at moments of anxiety. A repressed memory serves to reassure you that you're doing fine, that you can handle whatever comes up."

Lincoln looked at us suspiciously. "Are you sure my good luck belt didn't bring it on? I mean, I've had that feeling before, but not nearly as often as I've had it since I've been at camp."

"Maybe you've been more worried at camp than you are at home," Max suggested.

"I wouldn't blame you if you were," I said, pointing to the still faintly-green bruise on the side of his face. "Remember your pillow fight?"

"Yeah." All the excitement left Lincoln's face, and I felt bad for bursting his bubble.

"Hey, you figured out the riddle, though," I said, patting him on the back. "That's great. I haven't been able to figure it out yet, and I don't think any of the other kids have, either."

"That's right," Max said, nodding. "And if you can just hang on to the belt for four more days, you'll win our cabin a big party."

"Yeah." Lincoln smiled again.

"Why don't you two go on down to breakfast," I said, hoping they'd take the hint. "I want to sit here a while and enjoy the quiet."

Max nodded and they walked on down the road toward the cafeteria. A squirrel paused on a tree across the road and looked at me curiously. I probably looked pretty silly to him, a dumb girl perched on a tree trunk like an overgrown rat.

Some other girls passed by me, looking at me curiously, but I just smiled and said nothing. I didn't care what they thought. Some boys came out, too, but Ethan wasn't among them. I had just given up and started walking again when I saw Nick coming my way.

"Hey, Cassie, wait up," Nick called. I stopped. Maybe he'd tell me where Ethan was and I wouldn't have to ask.

"What's up?"

"I wanted to talk to you. Let's go on down to breakfast."

I looked around, but there was no sign of Ethan. "Uh, where's your sidekick this morning? Did you two have a fight?"

"No, Ethan just overslept. He's taking a shower." Nick glanced at me and I hoped my cheeks weren't as red as they felt. I'm not very good at being subtle.

"Actually, Cassie, that's what I wanted to talk to you about."

"What?"

"About you and Ethan."

I stopped walking. "There is no me and Ethan. I don't know what you mean."

Nick shook his head, exasperated. "Don't give me that. I know that you like him, and I know that he's interested in you, too."

He was? I could have kissed Nick, but I tried to be nonchalant. "So? I think he's interesting, that's all."

"He's not for you. Remember I told you I had a friend who all the girls go for? That's Ethan. He doesn't need any more girls. Leave him alone, will ya?"

I shook my head and started taking bigger steps. "I don't know what you mean, Nick Harris. I don't even like the guy."

Standing in the cafeteria line, the more I thought about what Nick said, the angrier I felt. What business was it of his who I talked to or hung around with? He wasn't my keeper, for heaven's sake. He wasn't my father, and for that matter, he wasn't even my full-fledged brother. He was my stepbrother, and he had no business telling me what to do.

Maybe he's just jealous, I thought, sitting down at an empty table. *Maybe he's upset because his good friend Ethan Wilcox wants to spend some time with me instead of all his time with Nick.* Nick probably couldn't understand why Ethan would want to spend some time with me, just an ordinary sister.

What was it Nick said? "I know that he's interested in you, too." What had Ethan told Nick? Had he asked about me? Said anything about me? Did he think I was pretty? I frowned. He probably thought I was a dweeb because I was always getting on him about smoking or cheating or something.

I took a sip of my orange juice and looked around. Ethan was interested in me! The other girls in my cabin would have a cow if they knew that of all the girls in camp, Ethan Wilcox was interested in me. Oh, he flirted with lots of them, but he was *interested* in me.

Maybe we'd get together this week and we'd fall in love and in a few years we'd get married. I'd straighten him out and he'd mature enough that he wouldn't do crazy things anymore, and we'd have beautiful children with Ethan's strong chin and dark eyes. Then we'd sit around and say, "Do you remember that spring at Camp Katumba?"

I'd laugh and say, "You were such a mess back then. I didn't think you would ever amount to anything. But this little flame of love began to grow, even though I couldn't stand the sight of you at first!"

He'd put his arm around me and say, "But I knew there was something special about you, sweetheart. I knew the minute I laid eyes on you that you were the one to change my life and make me happy—"

"I hope you weren't saving this for anyone."

I gulped. The Ethan Wilcox pulling out a chair to sit next to me now wasn't the Ethan of my dreams. He was real, his hair still wet from the shower, and he was so gorgeous I couldn't even find the words to start a simple conversation.

Ethan shook his milk carton, opened it, and

poured it over a bowl of Lucky Charms. "That old witch behind the counter nearly didn't let me through the line," he said, grinning at me. "Said I was late. I told her she'd be sorry if she didn't let me eat breakfast. So she let me in."

He wiggled his eyebrows at me and chugged a long drink from another carton of milk. I closed my eyes and shook my head. Why, oh why, did he have to be so *bad?*

"You shouldn't be rude to these people at camp," I told him, gently. "They're only trying to stick by the rules."

"Oh yeah." Ethan put down his milk carton and smiled at me. "You like rules, don't you, Cassie?"

I shrugged. "I guess. They keep us organized, don't they?"

"They keep us in boxes, you mean. Well, I don't believe in boxes. I want to be free. I think you should do what you want to when you want to do it."

I looked at him in confusion. "If we all did what we wanted to, this camp would be a mess," I pointed out. "People might drown if they swam without a lifeguard. People would be thrown from the horses if they didn't obey the trail guide." I pointed at his breakfast tray. "And no one would eat if the cafeteria workers didn't feel like coming in to work."

Ethan laughed. "Lighten up, Cassie. You need to

enjoy life more. Why don't you come out with me this afternoon?"

"After lunch?" I asked. I was mentally trying to visualize the camp schedule and see what Ethan meant. Did he want us to do something during today's free time?

"After lunch, during lunch, it doesn't matter," Ethan said. "But since you probably want to eat, OK, we'll do it after lunch."

"What are we doing?" I asked again, my curiosity kindled.

Ethan threw back his head and laughed. "Honestly, girl, you've got to get off this organization kick. Who knows what we'll do? We'll just do something, OK?"

"OK," I said finally, gathering my breakfast dishes on my tray. "I'll meet you here and we'll do something after lunch."

He was the only person still eating in the cafeteria when I left. Everyone else went back to clean their cabins, but apparently, the rules didn't apply to Ethan Wilcox. At least, he didn't think they did.

10

"Here she comes!"

The other girls in my cabin had seen everything, and when I came back to the cabin, they were waiting with their questions. "What was Ethan Wilcox doing at your table?" Meghann asked. "What did he say?"

"Don't you have a boyfriend at home?" Rachel asked. "What will he think about this?"

"Did he just sit with you because you're Nick's sister?" Emily asked. "Or does he want you to help him win that dumb belt from the little guys in the Beaver cabin?"

I took a deep breath. "I don't know why he sat with me," I began, "and we just talked. I have a friend at home who's a boy, Chip, and he doesn't own me. And Ethan could have sat with Nick if he wanted to, and no, I don't think he cares anything about winning that dumb Katumba belt from Max and Lincoln. Can we clean this cabin now?"

As we swept, emptied the garbage, made our bunks, and hung up our towels, the other girls kept up a steady stream of "I don't see why it has to be her" and "Ethan flirts with everyone, you know." I did my fair share of the cleaning and got out of there as fast as I could.

A lot of the boys were on the tree-shaded dirt road that led to the chapel already, and I joined them. As I looked around, though, there was no sign of Ethan or Nick, Max or Lincoln. I wondered where they were.

As we filed into the chapel, Meghann, Signe, and Sondra caught up to me and suddenly acted like my best friends. They saved a space for me in chapel, and once I sat down, they grinned and laughed and kept looking around to see if any "really fine" boys had come in. *They're probably hoping to get Ethan over here,* I thought, *or they're trying to break us up before we even get together.*

Ethan and Nick did come in finally, and Ethan looked over and smiled at me, but he sat with Nick. Nick didn't even look in my direction.

"What's going on?" Meghann asked, not very subtly. "Isn't Ethan going to sit with you?"

"Why didn't Nick look over here?" Signe asked. "Is he mad at you or something?"

"Shhhhh!" I shushed them and tried to listen to Doug Richlett's announcements. The Raccoon cabin was in first place in the overall competition, thanks to their outstanding performance in the lip-sync contest, but whoever ended up with the Golden Belt of Katumba would almost certainly win the entire competition and the free after-hours party on Saturday night.

That dumb belt, I thought. I looked around for Max and Lincoln, but they weren't in the chapel. I looked everywhere, but they weren't in their usual seats down front and they weren't in the back. It wasn't like Max to miss a meeting.

"Where's Max?" I whispered to Meghann. "Do you see him anywhere?"

Meghann shook her head, and I began to feel worried. What if the boy genius had started some experiment and hadn't been able to finish? Or what if he had an epileptic seizure? Would Lincoln know what to do?

Suddenly the quiet of camp was shattered by the piercing blast of an air horn. "That's the fire alarm," Doug told us. "Everyone to the lake."

Now I was really frightened. Even though they told us there would be a fire drill this week, I thought it was strange it came at a moment when Max and Lincoln were missing. Was it really only a drill?

We all filed out of the chapel and I was surprised to see people streaming toward the lake from other parts of the camp, too. The full-time cooks and maintenance crew came from the cafeteria, and the camp's caretaker came out of his house with his wife and kids. A group of boys came straggling from the direction of the boy's cabins, and behind them came Max and Lincoln.

"Max!" I called, half glad and half mad. I pushed through the throng of campers on the road and fell into step with him. "Where have you been? You weren't skipping the meeting, were you?"

"You won't believe what happened," Max said, doggedly jogging toward the lake with Lincoln behind him.

"Slow down and tell me, Max. Don't run, it's only a fire drill."

"Thank goodness," Lincoln said simply. "That's the luckiest thing that's happened to me today." I looked over at Lincoln and noticed that he wasn't wearing the Golden Belt of Katumba.

"What happened?"

"I'll tell you later, Cassie," Max told me, looking carefully around us at the other kids. "But not now."

We all stood around the lake for five minutes, then the fire alarm quit blaring and all was quiet. "Our morning meeting will resume in ten minutes," Doug yelled above the crowd. "I'll see you all there."

"Tell me now," I asked Max, and he nodded and we stepped off the road. Lincoln stood with us, pale and quiet.

"We had just finished cleaning our cabin," Max began, "when the boys from the Fox cabin came in and said they wanted to answer the riddle."

"So?"

"So Lincoln gave them the riddle: what goes on four legs in the morning, two legs at noon, and three legs in the evening. One guy answered and said it had to be a monkey."

"A monkey?" I laughed, then thought a minute. "Was that right?"

"No," Max went on.

"Then," Lincoln interrupted, "I said it was over, and they had to leave and try again later. But they wouldn't leave."

"In fact, one of the guys, Kyle Stickle, pulled out a knife," Max said, breathless. "He said they weren't going anywhere until they answered the riddle."

"They guessed everything—a squirrel, a kangaroo, a horse, an eagle, but none of them were right," Lincoln continued. "But I wasn't going to give up the belt even if they *had* gotten the right answer. It just wasn't fair."

"We were really scared," Max said, lowering his voice to a whisper. "And they said if we told anybody they'd come after us."

"They said they'd take us downstream in a canoe and dump us out," Lincoln said, his eyes as wide as golf balls. "We didn't know what to do."

"So what did you do?"

"Nothing. We just stood there stalling and then the fire alarm rang," Max said. "They took off like the voice of God had sounded."

"So—" I looked at Lincoln's jeans. "Where's the golden belt?"

"In a safe place," Lincoln said. "I don't want to wear it anymore. I'll let people answer the dumb riddle, but I don't feel like asking for trouble."

"Wow." No wonder the boys were scared. "What are you going to do? Are you going to tell Doug about this?"

Max shook his head. "No. It's only our word against theirs, and I don't want to make them mad. We don't have any proof they did anything wrong."

My stomach ached a little for Max. It must be terrible to be small and picked on by the older boys, and worse yet to have to suffer in silence. I didn't know if keeping quiet was the right thing to do, but I knew it would take guts just to walk through camp knowing that the boys from the Fox cabin were on the loose.

"At least there's one good thing," Lincoln said. "That belt brought us such good luck that the fire alarm rang just when we needed it. You can't have better luck than that."

I didn't have the heart to remind him that without his good luck charm the trouble would not have begun at all.

11

Lincoln and Max were still a little shaken even after the morning meeting, so I sat with them at lunch. We had just begun to enjoy our pizza when a shadow loomed over the table. "Get lost, little guys," Ethan said. "Today this is a table for two."

I closed my eyes—something in me didn't like Ethan bossing everyone around, but another part of me yearned for something as romantic and exciting as this. A table for two in the middle of camp—how sweet! And he did it for me.

"They've had a rough morning," I said after Max and Lincoln left. "I wish you hadn't done that, but thanks, anyway."

"What happened to the kiddies?" Ethan asked.

"I promised I wouldn't say," I answered. "But it shook them up pretty bad."

"Hey, if someone's messin' with them, you tell them to come see me," Ethan said, leaning back in his chair. He tossed his head. "Nobody will mess with them after that, I promise."

"Well . . . you could do me a favor and look out after Max and Lincoln." I knew I shouldn't mention it, but maybe Ethan could help. "Some boys in the Fox cabin pulled a knife on them today. They wanted to get that dumb golden belt."

Ethan raised an eyebrow. "Really? Say no more, Cassie. I'll handle it."

"Don't do anything," I begged, wishing I hadn't said anything. "Max said he wanted to handle it himself. Please don't do anything to make it worse."

Ethan just smiled at me. "Don't worry your pretty head, girl. Everything will be just fine."

We talked about school then, and Nick, and sports. "By the way," I laughed, "Nick doesn't really want me to hang around with you much."

"Why not?" Ethan seemed surprised.

"I don't know. Maybe he thinks I'm taking away his friend or something."

"Naw, he shouldn't feel that way," Ethan said, tilting his head toward me. "I mean, a guy's got to have guy friends, but a guy's got to have a girlfriend, too. You know what I mean?"

He smiled broadly and I noticed a dimple I hadn't seen before. "I know what you mean," I sighed.

I was hoping I'd get to spend the afternoon with Ethan, but he disappeared after lunch and I couldn't find him anywhere. I went down to the lake with a book again, but he wasn't on the blob or in the water. I went to the nature trail and sat on my reading rock, hoping he'd come by, but he didn't. I even walked up to the basketball court in the blindingly hot sun, but he wasn't up there, either. I suppose I could have asked Max and Lincoln to look for him in the circle of boys' cabins, but my pride wouldn't allow me to be that obvious. Yet.

At four o'clock I had nearly convinced myself that our fast-burning relationship was over, but he appeared out of nowhere and asked me to go horseback riding. "You're in the Bluebird Cabin, right?" he said. "So it's your turn to ride at four-thirty today. It's the Raccoon's time slot, too."

I had just enough time to run back to my cabin, throw on my jeans and a T-shirt, and meet Ethan by the road. We walked together across the fields to the barn where the horses were saddled and waiting. The trail guide put me on Jordache, a sturdy-looking black horse, and Ethan rode a beautiful light-stepping mare named Classy.

The trail ride was wonderful. Even though the

pace was slow, the trail led us through thick woods where huge spider webs gleamed in the sunlight. Our guide showed us deer tracks and alligator trails in the mud along the water. Outside on the playing fields and by the lake the sun was blisteringly hot, but under the canopy of trees along the riding trail, only pinpricks of sunlight came through.

Here, away from the other guys, Ethan seemed like a different person. He wasn't a smart aleck and he didn't show off. He was a good rider and seemed steady on his horse. As we rode side-by-side, I heard him speak to his mare softly. More than once he leaned down to pat her on the side. I don't know if it was the shade or the quiet, but Ethan seemed gentler somehow.

I didn't want him to think I was snooping, but I was curious. I got up my nerve and casually asked, "So where were you all afternoon? I looked for you after lunch, but you disappeared."

Ethan grinned. "Oh, last night a couple of the guys and I went out after lights out and soaped some of the windows on the Otter cabin. Doug Richlett caught us and made us stay inside today for two hours."

"Why would you do that?"

Ethan caught a tree limb that was about to hit his head and held it until my horse safely passed by.

"Those guys got mud all over our front porch—that's why we didn't win cabin inspection. That's all."

He didn't seem to mind being grounded at camp. It was as though being stuck inside his cabin for two hours was a small penalty to pay for soaping cabin windows. I couldn't figure that out, but I admired his confidence. If I'd been caught sneaking around after lights out, I'd have felt so guilty I would have asked to go home.

After our ride Ethan and I walked back to the cabins and paused at the fork in the road that led to the boys' cabins on the right, girls' cabins on the left. "Well, I'll see you later," I said reluctantly, not wanting to leave him.

"At dinner," Ethan said, smiling. "And sit with me at the concert tonight, OK?"

"Sure." I practically floated back to the cabin. I took a shower to wash away the smell of horse, shampooed my hair, and put on a fresh shirt and pair of jeans. Camp was wonderful. Life was wonderful. And I had never met anyone like Ethan.

Rachel and Emily came in while I was changing. They were in their bathing suits and covered with goose bumps.

"I can't believe you two swam in that cold water," I said, laughing. "It was our cabin's turn to go horseback riding."

"We didn't want to spoil your date with Ethan," Rachel said, a little sarcastically. "That reminds me—Nick is down at the fork in the road. He said he wants to talk to you."

I zipped my suitcase shut. "Well, he can wait a while. I know what he's going to say and I don't want to talk to him."

"What do you think he's going to say?" Emily asked, her eyes gleaming with curiousity.

"He's going to tell me not to hang around Ethan," I answered, looking under my bunk for my tennis shoes. "I think he's jealous because I'm taking his best buddy away for a few hours."

Rachel giggled. "I'll keep Nick busy if you want me to," she said, arching an eyebrow. "Emily and I both will."

"You have my blessing," I said, tying my shoe-laces. I stood up and gave myself a last glance in the mirror. "Now I'm going to sneak down to the cafeteria through the woods. I'll count on you two to keep Nick off my back."

Emily and Rachel did their job. During the evening service they practically forced Nick to sit between them, which made it easier for Ethan to come and sit with me. Plus, whenever Nick looked over my way, Rachel or Emily would say something to bring his attention back to them. He only managed to glare in my direction five or six times.

After some music, Doug got up to speak, and I tried to listen. Really I did. I crossed my arms and stretched out my legs and tried to concentrate. Ethan crossed his arms, too, and he looked totally relaxed. *Good,* I thought. *Now that he's sitting with me, maybe he'll learn something from Doug.*

But I was startled when Ethan's fingers brushed my arm. His arms were still folded across his chest, and anyone looking at us wouldn't even know he was touching me, but he ran his fingers gently up and down the back of my arm. I shivered. It was a weird feeling.

I kept my arms crossed, too, but I made one of my fingers catch his—mainly to stop him from brushing my arm like that. But his finger curled around mine and held it tight. My face felt like it was smoldering, but I kept my eyes glued to Doug's face and tried to think about Doug's topic: finding God's will.

We went from holding fingers to lacing our fingers together. It was a little game—our fingers touched, then let go, then held each other, then flew away. He brushed my arm, I brushed his. All the while we sat like wooden Indians, facing the front, stone-faced. No one in the room knew what was going on but me and Ethan. It made me a little dizzy to think about it.

When Doug asked us to bow our heads and pray, Ethan grabbed my hand outright and held it. I felt how warm his hand was and wondered what it would be like to hold his hand forever. His hand was strong, and mine felt small and powerless in his grasp.

Ethan dropped my hand as Doug said, "Amen," and we stood up and pretended that nothing at all had happened. "I'll see you later at the evening concert," Ethan promised, then he walked off to join Nick and the other guys from the Raccoon cabin. I waited for Rachel and Emily and congratulated them on a job well done.

We three girls went to the snack shop. "By the way, I hate to burst your bubble," I told them, "but Nick's been talking about this girl named Jacklyn at your school. Who's she?"

Rachel pouted. "He likes Jacklyn Malinga?"

I laughed. "Yeah, but nothing he's tried has worked with her. She won't go out with him."

Emily smiled. "Then there's hope for us, Rachel. Don't worry, Cassie, Jacklyn's not his type, anyway. They are as opposite as two people can be."

I took a bite of my frozen Three Musketeers bar

and chewed it thoughtfully. "Yeah, but don't opposites attract?"

Rachel shrugged. "Sometimes, but those things don't last. I mean, the attraction might be there, but if you've got nothing in common, what's a couple going to do? Nothing!"

"Maybe you've got a point there." I took another bite of my candy bar and thought about me and Ethan. We didn't have anything in common, not really. If we were going to last, I'd have to find some common ground. And fast. Ethan Wilcox was going to have to change.

12

I was on my way to freshen up before the concert when Nick literally jumped out at me from behind a tree. I gasped, then let him have it: "How dare you jump out at me like that? Are you trying to give me a heart attack? Or maybe you'd just rather I ran screaming through the woods?"

"Hush, Cassie, I want to talk to you. I know you've been avoiding me, but I want you to listen to me now."

I leaned back against a tree by the side of the road. "All right, but make it quick. I'm meeting Ethan in fifteen minutes and I still have to go back to the cabin."

"Ethan's not for you."

I shrugged. "Is that all? You've said that before. I think you're just jealous."

"I'm not jealous. I'm just trying to watch out for you, that's all."

"I can take care of myself, thank you very much."

"OK, then—what about Chip?"

A pang of guilt flashed across my mind, but I dismissed it. "What about Chip?"

"Isn't he your boyfriend? Aren't you two-timing him? Would you be hanging around with Ethan if Chip had been able to come to camp?"

I made a face. "Nick, that's silly. Chip is just a friend and besides, Chip wouldn't want me to be all alone here at camp."

"There are lots of other people you could hang out with besides Ethan."

"Oh yeah?" I laughed a sarcastic *ha ha*. "Yeah, everybody was just standing in line to be my friend, Nick. I noticed you were really eager to do things with me. If it weren't for Max and Lincoln, I'd have given up and gone home after the first day."

Nick looked down at the ground for a moment. "Sorry," he muttered. "But you haven't been Miss Outgoing, you know."

That did it. "Are you finished?" I pushed myself off the tree and walked away, leaving Nick on the dusty road.

The concert that night was great. It was given by a local group called Sound Doctrine, and they sang contemporary Christian music that I really liked. Ethan liked it, too, I could tell, even though he kept asking when they were going to rip into heavy metal. I just smiled at him and patted his arm. He had to be kidding.

The lights were dim in the chapel while the group played, and Ethan didn't bother to play our little hidden hand-holding game. He took my hand out of my lap, laced his fingers through mine, and held my hand in his lap through the entire concert. I felt a little awkward at first, because all the other girls kept looking in our direction, but I got used to it. By the time Jane Richlett looked in our direction and dropped her jaw, I was able to look her in the eye and smile.

Why was everyone so surprised that Ethan and I were getting together? Sure, Ethan was kind of wild. But he wasn't *really* bad. Maybe I wasn't known for being rebellious or anything, but I'm certainly no Miss Perfect. If they were surprised because they thought I was going with Chip—well, there'd be plenty of time to prepare Chip for the rumors once I got home.

At the end of the concert, the lead singer for Sound Doctrine stood up. "We should all be growing to love each other," he said simply, "and friendships that have the Lord as their foundation will never fade. They will continue through all of earthly time and then into eternity. Isn't that great?"

The band then began to play a pretty, soft song about how friends were friends forever if the Lord was in their relationship. Everyone in the crowd stood up and laced their arms around each other. Ethan dropped my hand and put his arm around my shoulder, gripping me so tightly that Emily, who was on my other side, gave up trying to reach me.

I looked up at Ethan as we all sang the chorus together: "And a lifetime's not too long to live as friends." When the song was done, Ethan looked down at me, that delicious sparkle in his eyes, and I wondered what it would be like if he just stooped down and kissed me. The feeling was so strong, I was suddenly afraid he just might—so I turned my head away and started prattling about what a great concert it had been.

We walked along the road at the edge of the stream of campers who were all headed to their cabins and bed. Doug Richlett passed by us and called over his shoulder, "Cassie, Ethan, don't forget rule number three!"

"What was rule number three?" I whispered, not remembering anything Doug had said that first day of camp. It seemed like a month ago.

"I dunno." Ethan smiled at me. "Something about not messing around with Marlboros or makin' out."

I blushed then because I knew he was thinking about kissing me. Did he want to? Would he? In front of all these other people? We came to the fork in the road and lingered a moment. Would he kiss me here? No, Jane Richlett walked up and her flashlight flickered over our faces for a minute. "It's getting late, you two," she said lightly. "Come on, Cassie, I've got to count heads in five minutes."

"OK," I told her. "Be there in a minute."

I looked at Ethan. I could hardly see his face through the darkness and I couldn't tell what he was thinking. "I've got to go," I said, pulling my hand away from his. "See you tomorrow, I guess."

"Hey, Cassie." His voice was low and urgent, and he wouldn't let go of my hand.

"What?" I whispered.

"Meet me here after lights out."

I laughed, but then stopped when Ethan didn't laugh along. He was serious. I bit my lip. Could I sneak out? Should I sneak out?

"Are you serious?"

"Yeah. Meet me here, OK?"

"I can't."

"Try? At least try?"

I hesitated, then thought of how nice it would be

to have some time alone with Ethan. "OK, I'll try," I promised.

There was no way I would be able to sneak out. After Jane made sure all six of us were in, she locked the door and casually sat down in front of it. "There's good light here, so I'm going to read a while with my flashlight," she told us, smiling. "So take your showers, pray together, and get some sleep, girls. I'll see you in the morning."

I told Jane good night and lay on my bunk, still dressed. Maybe if she got tired and went to bed, I could slip out and meet Ethan. If I got caught, what was the worst thing that could happen? I'd never done anything to get in trouble before, so Doug would probably give me a lecture. The worst he could do was send me home.

I tried to stifle a yawn, but it slipped out. I was dead tired. As my body grew numb with sleep, I thought about what would happen if Ethan and I were caught outside, in the dark, together. Maybe Doug would come up, find us talking, and send us both home. We'd ride home together on the bus or whatever, and during the trip we'd really have a chance to talk with no interruptions. I'd get to *really* know Ethan, and then I'd understand him. I could help him change. We could fall in love.

The next thing I knew it was morning.

13

I felt so tired the next morning I could hardly move.
There were muscles in my legs that ached where I
had never ached before. "Why'd I ever go horseback
riding," I groaned, sitting up in my bunk. Ouch.
Even my tailbone was tender.

I pushed my hair out of my eyes and looked
around. Emily and Rachel were buzzing around like
little bees, and Signe, Sondra, and Meghann were all
still sleeping.

"Is it time for breakfast?" I whispered to Emily.

She laughed. "It's nearly eight o'clock. If you don't
hurry up, you'll miss breakfast entirely."

Jane rapped on our door and stuck her head into
the room. "Well, the tiredness has finally set in," she
said, grinning. "What happened to my early risers?

Come on, Meghann, wake up. Sondra, Signe, you'll miss breakfast if you don't get moving."

The three girls lay like logs in their bunks. Sondra covered her head with her pillow, and Meghann quietly stuck her face into her stuffed teddy bear.

I was tired, too, but I didn't want to sleep through breakfast. Ethan was out there (and Max and Lincoln and a lot of other people, I reminded myself), and I didn't want to miss a minute of camp.

I had just finished pulling on my shorts and shirt when a girl from the Cardinal cabin knocked on our door. "I've got a note for Cassie Perkins," she said, handing me a sheet of paper.

Rachel squealed. "Who's it from?" and Emily stopped brushing her teeth. "Is ith fromth Ethan?" she asked, her mouth full of toothpaste suds.

I opened the paper and glanced at the bottom. "Yes," I answered. I pulled the paper closer to me so the other girls couldn't read over my shoulder and curled up in a corner of my bunk. I couldn't believe what he had written:

After Date Evaluation Form
1. Her attire: no variety—she always looks great.
2. Perfume: delicate—doesn't choke you, makes you want to sit closer.
3. Promptness: she was waiting for me by the road.

4. Was she at ease? She wasn't at attention!
5. Is she real or a fake? She seems sincere.
6. Conversation? A+++, and she doesn't just preach at people, either.
7. Did I have a good time? Yes
8. Can she relate to my friends? Sure, one of them is her brother.
9. Would I go out with her again? YES
10. Did she meet me like she promised? No.

Score: 90 percent.

I could feel my eyes bugging out of my head. Honestly, I never dreamed Ethan Wilcox would come up with something like this! No one had ever written me a note like this, and as much as I wanted to, I couldn't show the other girls. They might realize Ethan had asked me to meet him after lights out.

"What'd it say?" Emily persisted. "Is it good or bad?"

"It's good, I think," I answered. I bit my lip and folded the page into a tiny square. "Anyway, it's personal."

"Oooohhhh, *personal*," Rachel said.

"What's personal?" Meghann sat up, her red hair falling around her face. "Was that note from Ethan?"

"Yes, and I've got to go," I said. I brushed my hair quickly and double-checked to make sure my mascara wasn't smeared or globby. Whatever else Ethan

Wilcox was, he was certainly a surprise to me. What would he do next?

He was waiting for me at the fork in the road. "Did you get my note?" he asked as I walked up.

I reached out and playfully pinched his arm. "Yes, and thanks! That was the cutest thing I've ever seen. I'm only disappointed that I didn't, you know." I rolled my eyes. "Well, I tried to come out last night, but I couldn't. Our counselor sat in front of the door."

Ethan threw back his head and laughed so loudly that a swarm of birds left a nearby tree. "That's OK," he said, taking my hand. "You can try for 100 percent tonight."

He practically pulled me down the road to the cafeteria, but something he had said made me uncomfortable. I couldn't quite figure out what it was, and after a while I gave up. The day was too pretty, and Ethan was simply too cute to worry about anything. It was going to be a great day.

Lincoln was wearing the Golden Belt of Katumba again at breakfast. "What's up, guys?" I asked, pulling out a chair for Max at the table where Ethan and I were eating.

"Oh, we're invited to sit with you today?" Max asked, sarcastically.

"Of course. I'm wearing my lucky belt," Lincoln said, slipping into a chair.

"Why are you wearing your belt?" I asked. "I thought you decided it was better to keep it put away."

"I wasn't getting any lucky breaks," Lincoln said, taking a bite of his bagel. "I was chosen last yesterday when we played softball. I did a horrible job in volleyball and we lost. Last night I fell in the dark and bruised my arm, plus I think I got 268 mosquito bites."

"Why don't you just wear mosquito repellent like everyone else?" I asked him. "I don't think bugs care anything about that golden belt."

Max rolled his eyes and jerked his thumb in Lincoln's direction. "He's absolutely convinced that belt has some kind of power," Max said. "I've tried telling him that's ridiculous, but he just won't listen."

"It's not the belt that has power," Lincoln disagreed. "It's just that when I'm wearing it I feel, well, kind of important. Good things happen then, Max. You have to admit they do."

Max just shook his head and Ethan raised his eyebrows and looked at me. "Can you believe these guys?" he said to me, grinning. He turned back to Max and Lincoln and smiled at them. "I just can't believe you little guys."

"They're not little guys," I said gently, trying to correct him. "Max is a young guy, and Lincoln is a short guy. But they're both going to grow, Ethan. Just give them time."

Ethan stood up and stretched lazily, reaching his arms toward the ceiling. I couldn't help noticing that Max and Lincoln both watched him silently, probably wishing they could be six feet tall like Ethan was.

"It's OK, guys," I whispered to them as I gathered my dishes on my tray. "You'll grow. I promise."

I took notes during the meeting in chapel that morning, partly because I wanted to set a good example for Ethan, partly because I didn't want everyone to think my hand was glued to his, and partly because I felt guilty. I hadn't really listened to a single lesson all week.

Doug's theme, as usual, was on finding God's will, but that morning he spoke on how to find God's will in love. "Some people think love is something that just zaps you like a lightning bolt," he said, driving his fist into his palm for emphasis. "But it's not. Love is more than we think. We say we love French fries, we love our dog, we love our cars, we love God, and we love our girlfriends. Are those kinds of love equal?"

Of course not, I thought. *But anyone can tell the dif-*

ference. I don't love my mom the same way I love my brother. And I don't love either of them the same way I love Ethan.

But did I really love Ethan? It was the first time the idea had crossed my mind, and I clicked my pen and thought about it. What was love? If love meant getting tingles down your spine, and watching someone's every move from across the room, and hoping that you'd just bump into them in a crowded camp, then I loved Ethan. But was that right? Was that love?

"True love can stand the test of time," Doug was saying. "True love is a commitment of the will that lasts when your emotions aren't keen on loving someone. When you don't feel loving, true love acts. When you don't feel lovable, true love supports you. God is the best example of true love, because he loves us no matter what we do or what we are."

I hoped Ethan was listening. I didn't know anything about his spiritual life, but I didn't think Ethan was really living for God.

I wrote "Love stands the test of time" in my notebook. Ethan watched me write it, then casually took my pen out of my hand. It was a nice gold pen, one of many we have around the house, because Tom gives them to his clients. They're all engraved with "Thomas Harris, Esquire."

"Nice pen," Ethan whispered, handing it back to me.

"Thanks," I whispered back. "They're everywhere at my house."

"Really?" Ethan raised an eyebrow. "I sure could use one." Without a word I handed him my pen. He smiled and looked a little embarrassed, but then he stuck it in his pocket. Rats. I was hoping he'd follow my example and take notes on what Doug was saying.

"God is molding you, right now, to be the kind of person you need to be for the person you will one day marry," Doug said. "So guard your thoughts and your actions. Pray that God will bring you through the situations that lie in your future so that you will be strong for your true love."

It all sounded so romantic. Maybe all the stuff I had gone through with my parents' divorce was just to make me strong for someone like Ethan. I had learned to be tough, and Ethan would need a strong woman. Maybe this was part of God's plan, but how could I be sure?

I knew what my mother would say. First, she'd probably laugh at the idea that I was in love. Then she'd say I was too young, because tenth grade girls just don't go off and fall permanently in love. But weren't Romeo and Juliet supposed to be fourteen and fifteen? Didn't Doug once say that Mary, the

116

mother of Jesus, was probably thirteen or fourteen? My own grandmother got married when she was sixteen.

I'd have to show Mom. Maybe she wouldn't let me get married or anything, but she couldn't stop my feelings. My love was a steadily burning flame, and nothing would be able to put it out. Didn't Doug say that true love was tough? My love for Ethan would last no matter what came our way.

14

We went swimming together after lunch. The water was still freezing and my teeth chattered the whole time, but when Ethan put his hands around my waist to lift me and remarked how small my waist was, I felt so warm inside I could have stayed in for hours.

After swimming, we went to our separate cabins and put on shorts. We went for a walk down the nature trail, trying to find a place to be alone, and finally we came to my reading rock, which was enough off the path that we could have some privacy. Ethan stretched out on the rock, exposing his face to the sun, and I sat beside him, hugging my knees.

"Tell me about your family," I said, wanting to know everything about him.

"Not much to tell," Ethan said, his eyes closed against the sun. "My father's a jerk. He beats my mother a lot. He used to beat my sister and me all the time, too, until I got big enough to stop him." He gritted his teeth and even though he was trying to relax, I could see that thinking about his father made him tense.

"Why doesn't your mother leave?" I asked.

"Dunno," Ethan answered. "She just says she can't. I don't know why, though, 'cause I'd take care of her."

My heart broke then for Ethan, and it was all I could do not to scoop him up in my arms and hold him. How terrible it must have been to grow up in his family! My parents had fought and gotten a divorce, but my father *never* hit my mother. The only time Max or I ever got hit was when we got a well-deserved spanking, and we always knew that Mom and Dad loved us.

"I'm sorry," I said, reaching out to gently touch his arm. "I'm just so sorry."

"It's OK," Ethan brushed my hand away. "I can take care of myself. I take care of Mom and Crystal, too. I just ignore anything Dad says, and then I do what I think is right."

A lot of things about Ethan began to make sense. No wonder he didn't care anything about rules. He never obeyed any of his father's rules, so why should he obey anyone else's?

"You ought to just pretend it never happened," I said, trying to help him feel better. "Everyone in the world isn't like your dad. There are lots of really nice people in the world who want to help you. Like Nick and—"

"Like Doug Richlett?" Ethan sat up, shading his eyes from the sun. "Man, that guy's always on my case about something. He's threatened to send me home five times."

"Like me, Ethan. I want to help you." Ethan just grinned at me and lay back on the rock. I was glad he had confided in me and I felt as protective as a mother bear. "You can't be comfortable," I told him. "Put your head in my lap."

With his head in my lap, Ethan actually went to sleep. I sat there for a long time, listening to the birds and the faraway noise of the kids playing in the lake, and I thought a lot about Ethan. Nobody was going to do anything to Ethan if I could help it. He'd been through enough, and I was going to try to make things better. Wouldn't God want me to help as much as I could?

When he finally woke up I was glad we could move on. Sitting still on that hard rock had done nothing to help my stiff muscles.

We came out where the nature trail ended on the main road and saw Max and Lincoln hurrying toward their cabin. Both boys were dripping wet, and Lincoln was covered with a fine layer of dirt. Tears had streaked fine lines down his cheeks.

"What's wrong?" I asked.

"Kyle Stickle and his buddies from the Fox cabin tipped our canoe in the middle of the lake," Max said, sputtering. "I lost everything in my pockets, plus Mildred floated away."

"Mildred? Your gerbil?"

Max nodded. "She was in her little container, and she floated out of reach. But by the time we got the canoe right-side-up and empty, she was gone." Max looked like he was about to cry. "I just hope she can get out, or she'll starve to death."

"Or drown," Lincoln added. He glared up at me and Ethan. "So when we got back to the shore, I lit into one of those guys."

"What happened then?" I asked.

Lincoln looked down at the ground, and Max explained: "Doug Richlett came out and stopped the fight. It's a good thing, too, because Lincoln was los-ing."

"At least I tried!" Lincoln glared at Max. "You just stood there!"

"I don't like to fight," Max said evenly, his brown

hair dripping. "I'm smart enough to know fighting doesn't solve anything."

They were about to fight themselves, so I interrupted. "You two need to go change clothes," I said, stepping between them. "Then you can walk along the bank and look for Mildred. But you'd better hurry up. It'll be dinnertime soon, and then it will be dark. So hurry!"

As they walked off, waving their arms and still yelling at each other, Ethan looked at me with a wicked sparkle in his eye. "I'll take care of those Fox boys for you, Cassie," he said, smiling. "Just wait and see."

"You don't need to do anything," I assured him. "Max and Lincoln didn't drown, so I guess they're OK."

Ethan laughed. "I guess that golden belt didn't do anything to help that unlucky gerbil!"

After the evening meeting, Camp Katumba offered its traditional skit night. Each cabin was to present a skit, and the girls in my cabin had some crazy idea about dressing up like an elephant and then dropping water on some poor unsuspecting victim.

"You ask for a volunteer from the audience," Sondra explained. "Then the ringmaster warns the volunteer that the elephant is very nervous."

"Very nervous," Signe echoed.

"We did this last year," Meghann added. "And it's a riot. First you have the elephant count to three by stomping his feet. Rachel, if you're the front end, you stomp twice, and Emily, if you're the back end, you stomp once."

"I don't want to be the back end." Emily sniffed.

"It's cute," Signe assured her. "We cover you both with a sheet and you hold a hairbrush out from under the sheet for a tail. Rachel will hold her hand out the front end to be the trunk."

"I'll be the ringmaster," Meghann said, "and Sondra and Signe will be my assistants. That leaves Cassie." She looked at me. "What can you do?"

The last thing in the world I wanted to do was to be in their dumb skit. I wanted to sit with Ethan in the audience and just watch.

"You can leave me out of this," I said, rereading my after-date evaluation form. "I'll pass."

"What a party pooper," Sondra said, raising her nose in the air. "Just because you've got a boyfriend, all of a sudden you're too good to be with us."

"It's not that," I tried to explain, "it's just—"

"We don't need her anyway," Meghann said, turning her back to me. "She can't be the volunteer because she knows the joke. Anyway, here's what we do. The elephant walks over to the volunteer the first time OK, then the second time, Sondra, you make a loud noise and Rachel, you spill the water on the person so it looks like the elephant had to go to the bathroom and—"

They all squealed.

What a dumb idea. I left them alone and went for a walk.

That night I grew angrier with every passing skit. I had deliberately stayed out of my cabin's skit so I could sit with Ethan, but he was so excited about being in his cabin's lip-sync version of "Good Vibrations" that he stayed with the guys all night. He didn't even sit with me, and, as usual, I was alone.

Some of my anger faded, though, when he and his group got up to sing. He was so irresistibly *cute* up there, playing his invisible air guitar and singing, "I'm digging those good vibrations. She's giving me ex-ci-tations." Nick was good on the invisible set of drums, too, and I wasn't surprised when their cabin won the award for best skit. The applause meter went *way* off the scale when we voted by clapping for our favorites. My fellow Bluebirds came in sixth place with that dumb elephant skit. It was poor Doug Richlett who volunteered and got soaked.

Since Ethan hadn't looked at me all night, I was ready to slip out into the darkness and go to my cabin, but I heard him call me: "Hey, Cassie, wait up." He ran down the aisle of the hall and took my hand. "Let me walk you home, lovely lady."

My anger vanished and I laughed as we stepped out into the cool night air. It really was much cooler up in north Florida than it was at home, and the thought of going home in just two more days made a lump rise in my throat. But Ethan did live close by and even though we went to different schools it wouldn't be too hard to see him after camp was over. Plus, he and Nick were good friends.

I was thinking about how I could see him at home when Ethan pulled me off the road and into the shadow of the trees. Before I even knew what was happening, he bent and kissed me.

At first it felt a little strange to feel his lips on mine, but I decided to ignore the strangeness. I reached out and tangled my fingers in his hair. He pulled me closer to him, kissed me harder, and then let me go.

"Oh, Ethan," I said, not knowing what else to say.

"See if you can come out tonight," he said, as if that kiss was only a promise of what could follow. "But if you can't, flash your lights on and off. I'll see it."

He walked away then, a little abruptly, and I hurried toward my cabin. I would try my hardest to come out tonight. There was no way I was going to sleep after a kiss like that.

I don't know how she knew; maybe she has antennae in the back of her head. But somehow Jane Richlett must have known I wanted to go out. She didn't say anything unusual, and I didn't either, but she called us together before lights out and sat us in a circle. "I know camp is a great time to be away from your usual routines," she said, smiling at us. "But I want you to remember we want you to come apart during this week so you can think about and learn about what God has planned for you. That is the most important part of camp."

I felt a familiar twinge of guilt again. What had I learned about God? Not much. I'd spent all my time trying to learn about Ethan Wilcox.

"So tonight I want each of you to spend some private time in prayer before you go to bed," Jane said. "I'll be in my bed, too, and I'm going to trust you all to do this. Let's just spend some time thinking about whose we really are."

That did it. We all got up out of the circle and got ready for bed. I slipped out of my shorts, pulled on my nightgown, and gave the light switch a very definite off-on-off flash before lying down on my bunk. Ethan might never understand why I couldn't come out when the warden wasn't even guarding the door, but Jane had asked us to do something and there was no way I could think about God and Ethan's kiss at the same time.

15

I know every female in camp watched me at breakfast on Friday morning because I was the only girl at a table full of boys: Ethan, Nick, Max, Lincoln, and a couple other Raccoons.

Max and Lincoln were in a somber mood. Last night, Max told me, they found Mildred's temporary container by the bank. She had escaped, somehow, and was now roaming the woods, a free gerbil.

"At least you know she didn't drown," I said with a shrug. "She'll be fine, Max. Don't worry about her."

"At least she wasn't with a male gerbil," Lincoln pointed out. "So she can't reproduce and ruin the ecosystem."

I laughed. Lincoln and Max really were a lot alike. And Camp Katumba was safe from a gerbil invasion, unless, of course, some other kid lost a male gerbil at camp last week.

It was a nice breakfast until Kyle Stickle and a couple of boys from the Fox cabin stopped at our table and glared at Lincoln long enough for him to squirm. Ethan noticed. "Hey, you twerps had better move along," he said smoothly. "Or you'll be sorry."

They did, but not before Kyle told Lincoln: "Enjoy it while you can, bud, because you're not winning any party."

"Kyle, you can acquire the belt if you want it," Max said. "All you have to do is answer the riddle."

Kyle glared and moved away, and Ethan laughed. "Hey, Max, what is the answer to that riddle, anyway?"

Max grinned and shook his head. "No way."

Ethan looked at me. "Do you know?"

I shook my head, too. "I don't know. And Max won't tell me, either."

Ethan laughed and chugged down the rest of his milk. Just then Doug Richlett walked over. "Well, Cassie, how does it feel to be the only camper who gets mail all week?" He handed me a postcard.

Bewildered, I read it:

Hi Cassie!
Hope you're having a great time. I'm really sorry I couldn't be there with you, but I know God wants you to learn something special this week. See you soon. I miss you! —Chip.

I read the card and casually tucked it in my pocket. I thought maybe Ethan wouldn't notice, but he did.

"Good news from home?" he asked casually.

I shrugged. "Just a note from a friend."

Ethan raised an eyebrow. "A boyfriend?"

"Chip is a boy, yes, and a friend. That's all."

"Oh." Ethan stirred his cereal absently, then cleared his throat and looked around at the other guys. "Who wants to take my tray up today?"

They quietly looked at each other, then Lincoln sighed and volunteered. "I'll do it, I guess."

I couldn't believe Ethan got other people to do his dirty work for him. I picked up my tray, and Ethan offered, "Want me to get someone to take your tray, Cassie?"

"No, I'll take it myself," I said gently. Ethan had a lot to learn, and I could start teaching him by being a good example.

After lunch we were allowed to sign up for a special advanced horseback trail ride. Ethan and I signed up, so did Max, Lincoln, Nick, Sondra, Signe, and Meghann. Rachel and Emily said they had horses of their own, so horseback riding on a trail was nothing but boring to them.

We mounted our horses and Manuel, our trail guide, led us down the familiar path through the woods. "When we reach the empty pasture on the other side of these trees, we'll let you gallop," he promised. "Until then, though, give your horse free rein and let him walk. It's too dangerous to let the horses run in the woods." He grinned. "We've lost a couple of campers that way."

"What does he mean, he's lost campers?" I leaned over and whispered to Ethan.

"Don't worry, Cassie," Ethan said, handling his horse well. He would make a good-looking cowboy, I decided. "If you fall off, I'll pick you up."

He was teasing, so I laughed at him and kicked my horse gently in the ribs so she'd move ahead of his horse. Fall off, indeed. I'd never fallen off a horse, and I wasn't about to start now.

Up ahead, on a pitiful-looking short horse that actually was a large pony, Lincoln was still wearing the Golden Belt of Katumba. "Hasn't anyone guessed the riddle and taken that belt from you yet?" I called out to him. "Or hasn't anybody tried?"

"Oh, lots of people have tried," Lincoln said, looking back and smiling proudly. "But no one's guessed the riddle. They've guessed horses, and spiders . . . "

"Kangaroos and koalas," added Max, swaying with the gentle rhythm of his horse's steps.

"Fish and toys and tractors," Lincoln said. "You

name it, they've guessed it. But no one's gotten the right answer yet."

"And you're still wearing it." I shook my head, a little surprised that someone would want to wear a golden belt for an entire week.

"Why not wear it?" Lincoln asked. "Everyone has to let me go first when I'm wearing it. Plus, I'm convinced it really is bringing me good luck."

"We'll see about that," I said, pulling in my reins. Ethan had allowed himself to fall behind, and I wanted to ride beside him. I waited until the other riders had passed, then my mare fell into step with Ethan's horse. "Having fun?" I asked him.

"Sure," he said, but he looked slightly bored. I smiled and tried to cheer him up. "When we get to the field, do you want to race?"

Ethan looked at me, and his expression was blank. "Why wait?" he said suddenly. Without warning, he kicked his horse in the ribs and it shot off like a rocket.

I couldn't move. Ethan's horse tore past the others, nudging the surprised horses off the trail and spooking more than a few. As Ethan tried to pass Lincoln's pony, the pony flattened his ears and kicked his hind legs into the path of Max's horse. Max's horse reared and whinnied, Ethan's horse kept plunging ahead, and Lincoln's frightened pony took off in a dead gallop through the woods.

The pony passed a startled Manuel, who turned sideways and blocked the trail. "You all stay right here!" he barked, then he whirled on his mount and took off after Lincoln.

Ethan stopped his horse and sat high in the saddle laughing. "Isn't that a kick?" he said, watching the tree limbs ahead of us bend and shimmy. "Did you see that pony roll his eyes back in his head? Good ol' Lucky Lincoln will have a time reining in that horse, let me tell you!"

"Ethan, that wasn't funny!" For once I wasn't worried about being gentle.

"Oh, these horses know the trail," Ethan said smoothly. "He'll just gallop along until he gets tired, then he'll calm down. As long as Lincoln hangs on, he'll be fine."

I wasn't so sure. We were at the top of a hill, and I could see another section of the trail down below us, so I dismounted and pulled my horse over to the edge to try to catch a glimpse of Lincoln.

Sure enough, I heard the pounding of hoofs below, and Lincoln and Manuel came into view. Lincoln was as stiff as a toy soldier, with his eyes closed and both hands firmly on the horn of his saddle. His reins flapped wildly against the horse's front legs. Manuel was trying to stay next to Lincoln, but the trail was narrow and the tree limbs slapped his face and tore at his clothes. With one quick move, Manuel's trained horse forced Lincoln's pony off the trail and steered him toward the trees, so the frightened animal made an abrupt right turn, throwing Lincoln into the bushes.

We heard a long, high scream, and then nothing. The dazed pony stood there, panting heavily. Manuel rode his lathered horse to the edge of the trees and peered down into the bushes. "Hey, kid?" he called. "You all right?"

"I'm fine," Lincoln called. He stood up, brushed himself off, adjusted his golden belt, and wobbled out of the bushes. Up on the top of the hill, we all cheered.

Manuel grinned at him. "You want to ride your horse back up?" he asked. "Or do you want to ride with me?"

Lincoln gulped and tilted his head. I knew he'd give anything to just ride behind Manuel for the rest of the trip, but his pride wouldn't let him.

"I'll get back on my own horse," he said weakly. "But I don't want to gallop when we reach the pasture, OK?"

"OK," Manuel said with a grin. He held the pony's reins while Lincoln shakily climbed back on, then the subdued pony and Lincoln climbed back up the trail toward the rest of us.

16

After that long and horsey ride, I needed a shower. I told Ethan I'd see him later, because I wanted to go to my cabin and clean up.

"OK," Ethan said, winking at Nick. "Nick and I wanted to go swimming, anyway."

"Ugh." I shuddered. "Maybe I'll just stay in and relax while you guys swim. I still can't get used to that cold water."

As I left him, Ethan pulled me to him and gave me a quick kiss. I was embarrassed, because I thought Doug Richlett would have a fit if he found out, but the only person who saw was Max.

"Come on, Max," I said, stretching my legs so they'd feel normal again. (Why do your legs feel so weird after being on a horse?) "I'll walk you back to the cabin road."

"No, thanks," Max answered coolly. He frowned at me. "I'll walk with Lincoln."

What was his problem? I tried to figure it out, then shrugged. He probably just wanted to give Lincoln some moral support after his spill from the horse. I watched the two of them walk away and shook my head. Whatever Max's problem was, I hadn't done anything wrong, so I wasn't going to worry about it.

Rachel and Emily were asleep on their bunks when I got back to the Bluebird cabin, so I took a quiet, quick shower. As I stood in the shower with the cool water spilling over me, I laughed aloud. What a week it had been. Just a few days ago I had been bored and lonely, and now it looked as though God had brought excitement and real romance into my life. Ethan wasn't exactly what I had thought I'd fall for one day, but he was never boring!

I got out of the shower and got dressed. Through the bathroom door I could hear Meghann, Signe, and Sondra in the next room. "Are you going to tell her?" Meghann asked. "Someone should tell her."

"I'm not going to tell her," Sondra said.

"Well, I don't want to tell her," Signe said. "Why don't we just show her?"

I didn't know what they were talking about, but I put my finger across my lips when I opened the bathroom door. "Shhhh," I warned them, pointing to the bunks. "Rachel and Emily are sleeping."

Meghann looked at me and narrowed her eyes in thought. "Cassie, come outside for a minute," she said. "We think you should know about something."

What was this? I stepped outside, my towel still in my hand, and looked around. "Know about what?" I asked.

"Come on down to the lake," Signe said, leading the way. "This will only take a minute."

Whatever it was, I was sure it was dumb. What could it be? Was Max conducting some crazy experiment with Lincoln? Was Nick trying to bribe the cabin inspector?

We went to the lake through the field, not by the road, and standing at the crest of a hill I could see all the activity on the shore. "Just look," Meghann said, pointing down to the lake. "Tell us what you see."

I squinted and looked carefully. Max and Lincoln were down at the canoe dock, wrestling with a canoe three times their size. That was nothing unusual. Nick was over at the slide, standing in line with several friends from the Raccoon cabin. That was no big deal. I saw Kyle Stickle and some of those troublemaking boys from the Fox cabin on a huge inner tube in the middle of the lake, but they weren't doing anything wrong or the lifeguard would have made them come out of the water.

"What?" I asked, looking at Meghann. "Why'd you bring me out here?"

"You're looking in the wrong place," Sondra said. "Look down there—under the tree."

I squinted again. On the shore of the lake was a large, sprawling oak tree, and under the tree was a large blanket where two kids were lying out to get some sun. It was a guy and a girl, and the guy was rubbing suntan lotion on the girl's back.

"Who is that girl?" I asked, not quite able to see that far.

"That's Vallie Walton," Sondra said. "She's gorgeous, and she goes to my church."

"She's in the Heron cabin," Signe added.

"OK, so?" I asked, looking again. "Who's the guy?"

The guy stopped rubbing lotion on the girl's back and turned his head in our direction. I gasped. It was Ethan.

Meghann nodded smugly when she heard my reaction. "We thought you'd like to know. They've been down there, all cozy, for over an hour."

Over an hour? That meant Ethan kissed me good-bye, ran to his cabin, changed his clothes, and practically ran to the lake and jumped on Vallie Walton's blanket. That meant he couldn't *wait* to leave me at the horses. How long had he been looking at Vallie Walton? What was going on here, anyway?

I spun on my heel and left, not wanting to give Meghann and her friends the satisfaction of seeing me get upset. I would just go in my cabin and stay there, maybe I'd even write Chip a letter. It'd serve Ethan Wilcox right if he got the sunburn of his life.

17

Our fight was not a pretty scene. Meghann and her friends arranged it all. They waited until Ethan and Vallie walked up the cabin road, then they pulled Ethan off to the side and told him I wanted to see him. Right away.

Ethan shrugged. "Maybe later. I need to change."

"Cassie needs to see you *now*," Sondra said. "She's really mad."

Ethan grinned confidently at them. "OK, so where is she?"

"Right over there," Meghann said, pointing to the picnic table where I sat in the shade, watching everything.

"Hey, Cass, what's up?" Ethan said, slinging his towel over his shoulder and coming toward me.

"What's wrong? Why'd you have to send the goon squad after me?"

I quietly blew air through my teeth, feeling like I would explode. It wasn't going to be easy, confronting Ethan. I was so mad I knew I could burst into tears at any moment.

"I just wanted to know why you were so chummy down at the lake with that Vallie girl," I asked, trying to keep my voice light and steady. "That's all."

"That?" Ethan propped one leg on a bench of the picnic table. "She's just a good friend, that's all. You were tired, and I knew you didn't want to swim." He looked down at me and raised an eyebrow. "Can't I have a friend who's a girl?"

Was this about Chip? Was he upset because I got that postcard from Chip?

"Of course you can have friends," I said, looking up into his eyes. They were impossible to read, so I looked away and waved my hands in confusion. "It just looks bad, that's all. Meghann and her friends saw you two down there being all cozy and all, and they just thought it looked like—"

"Like what?"

"Well, like you were two-timing me or something."

Ethan laughed. "I didn't know we were going steady."

144

His words were like a whip across my heart. "We're not," I faltered, "but I thought you really—"

"I like you, Cassie, I really do," Ethan said, swinging around. He sat next to me on the picnic bench, dangerously close. He put his hand on my knee and held it there while his other hand turned my face toward his. "I guess I just didn't know how you felt about me. I mean, twice I've asked you to meet me at night, and you haven't come. Now what am I supposed to think? If I like a girl, *nothing's* going to stop me from meeting her."

Hadn't I shown him how I felt? Couldn't he see that I had done nothing but think about him for the last three days?

"I care about you, Ethan," I whispered. "And I'm sorry I didn't come out, but I didn't think I could. I'll try again tonight, if you want, but I just don't know if I'm doing the right thing. I don't feel right about breaking the rules."

"If you really care about a person, you'll do anything to prove it," Ethan said slowly. He gently ran his finger from my forehead to the tip of my nose. "But I don't want you to do anything you don't want to do. Now I've got to go change. I'll see you at dinner."

He gave my knee a quick squeeze, then got up and walked toward the boys' cabins. Meghann, Sondra, and Signe came running over, squealing that everything was all right because they'd seen the whole thing, and I gave them a confident smile. But in the depth of my heart I wondered: Was everything all right?

The campground was quiet in the half hour before dinner because almost everyone was in their cabins changing clothes or resting. It felt good to walk around the grounds alone. I had time to think and plan and dream.

Poor Ethan. I had never met anyone so insecure. That had to be why he was always so mouthy and trying to be the center of attention. From what he'd told me I was sure he never got any positive attention at home, so he tried to get it any way he could. He needed love and understanding and someone who would stick up for him. I could give him those things. I could be the someone he needed.

A familiar figure was coming up the road, and I knew in an instant it was Max. He was walking with his hands in his pockets and his face toward the sky, and I knew he was thinking hard about something. Max will be an absentminded-professor type when he's old, unless he marries some lively girl who keeps him on his toes. Maybe in a few years I'd set Max up with one of my girlfriends. Now that I was in love, I wanted everyone to be in love.

"Hi, Whiz Kid," I called, walking in his direction. "Got a minute?"

Max snapped out of his daze and looked at me. "I don't know you," he said simply. "Go away."

I stared at him in amazement—and hurt. "What on earth is wrong with you?" I snapped impatiently. "Come down to earth, Max, and talk to me. Why were you so nasty to me today after the trail ride?"

"You kissed Ethan Wilcox, right there in front of everybody," Max said, thrusting his chin in my direction. "I can't believe you did that."

"Would you rather I kissed him in private?" I said, trying to joke. "Or is it just the thought of Ethan you can't stand?"

"Cassie Perkins, you've lost your mind," Max muttered, ignoring me and walking on. "Ethan Wilcox is a certifiable creep."

"You seem to like him well enough when he's keeping those jerks in the Fox cabin away from you and Lincoln."

"OK, so bullies serve their purpose. But I can't believe you'd kiss him. Have you gone crazy?"

"I think I love him," I whispered.

Max slapped the side of his forehead and looked up at the skies. "Are you hearing this, God?" he called loudly. "Can you figure this one out? 'Cause I sure can't."

"Shut up, Max." I was about to clamp my hand over his mouth. "You can't understand it because you've never been in love. It's not something you plan, it just happens. Ethan needs me."

"He needs a parole officer."

"He needs help. His father beats him."

Max shook his head. "That doesn't matter. You're not a social worker, Cassie. I thought you were a girl who cared about your reputation. I thought you were trying to live like a Christian."

"I am!"

"Not this way, you're not. Ethan Wilcox has a terrible reputation. You've even seen some of the things he's done. But you still kissed him in broad daylight! Do you know what people are going to say about you?"

"They're not going to say anything," I said, kicking the ground in frustration. "I don't care what Ethan has done with other girls—I'm not that way. I'm going to help him."

"Who's going to help you when he's through with you?" Max yelled. I was surprised to see there were tears in his eyes. He gulped, took a deep breath, and went on. "You're being really stupid, Cassie. You're letting your heart tell you you're in love, but your head is on vacation. Love is more than emotions. It's an intelligent decision based upon common ground, common goals, and common commitments."

Leave it to Max to make something as romantic as love sound like a mathematical formula. "You're only eleven years old," I muttered, crossing my arms. "What do you know about it?"

Max shrugged. "I've seen Mom and Dad get divorced. I've seen Mom fall in love again. I think I'm in a good position to evaluate what is love and what isn't."

"You don't know about this," I said, trying to explain. "Love is like a fire. It starts small, with a single flame, then it grows and then—"

"Remember what Shakespeare said in *Richard II*," Max warned.

I had no idea what he meant. "What did Shakespeare say?"

"Violent fires soon burn out themselves," Max recited.

I gazed at him blankly. "So?"

"This is a violent fire, Cassie," Max said. "And you'll get burned if you're not careful."

"You're just a kid," I told him, walking away. "Just a twerpy little kid, even if you can quote Shakespeare."

18

During the evening service Doug spoke on finding God's will again. I really wanted to listen tonight, because after thinking about what Max said, I wanted to be sure that Ethan was God's will for me.

Doug read Proverbs 3:5-6: "Trust in the Lord with all your heart and lean not on your own understanding; in all your ways acknowledge him, and he will make your paths straight."

"'Trust in the Lord,'" Doug told us. "Not just believe in the Lord, but trust in him. Know that he has your best interest at heart, and lean on him, not on your own understanding."

Trust in the Lord, I wrote in my notebook. I elbowed Ethan and scrawled *Why don't you take notes? You've got my favorite pen!* But he just smiled and shook his head. A few minutes later, I noticed

his eyes were closed. He was sound asleep! Well . . .
it *had* been a long day. . . .

I sighed, and Doug Richlett went on. "Notice that
we aren't supposed to lean on our own understanding. But we are supposed to use it," he said. "God
gave you a brain for more of a reason than to take
up space between your ears. He wants you to use
your understanding, your common sense. But when
it comes down to making a tough decision, rely on
him."

What Doug was saying sounded vaguely familiar.
Max would agree with Doug, I realized, because Max
used his brain for everything. Had I been using
mine? Had I really thought about Ethan and this
relationship, or had I just been carried along?

"'In all your ways, acknowledge him,'" Doug said,
smiling at us. "When you have to make a decision
and you want to know God's will, ask yourself, 'Can
I honor and please Jesus Christ by doing this?' If you
can, then it is probably God's will. But if you can't,
you'd better stop and reevaluate."

Could I honor and please Christ in my relationship with Ethan? I frowned. Sure I could. Didn't God
want me to help him? Ethan certainly needed help.
Of course, I hadn't really been very outspoken about
my relationship with Christ, and I hadn't really
talked to Ethan about God . . . but I would. In time.

"And he will make your paths straight," Doug said, reading from his Bible. "Paths are for walking. If you trust in the Lord and lean not on your own understanding, if you acknowledge him in all your ways and set out on a path, God will show you his will. He'll let you know if you're on the right path."

Doug put his Bible down on a table and seemed to look right at me. "There is a time for praying about what to do, and there is a time to get up and start walking. If you need to know God's will right now, you should pray, then act carefully. God will show you what to do."

Could it be that simple? Maybe it could. While Ethan slept and Doug talked on, I closed my eyes and prayed silently. *Dear God,* I prayed, *I really love Ethan. I want to help him know you like I do, and I want to help him when he needs help. Please, Lord, show me clearly what I am to do. I will trust you in this, and I'll try to use my understanding.*

There. I had prayed. Now, according to Doug, it was time to start walking and acting carefully.

After the service, Ethan and I went to the snack shop for a Coke. The sun was setting over the lake, and we sat on top of a picnic table to watch it sink behind the trees. It was a beautiful, romantic setting.

"What's the activity tonight?" Ethan asked, interrupting the mood. "I never look at my schedule."

I pulled out my notebook. "It's some game called mission impossible. It says here we should wear our grubbies again."

Ethan leaned closer and I felt his shoulder press into mine. "I don't feel like running around in the dark," he said, his dark eyes scanning my face. "Do you?"

A mosquito droned in my ear and I was tempted to reach up and slap it off, but I didn't want to break Ethan's concentration on me. "Not really," I murmured. "But what else is there to do?"

Ethan looked off into the distance and jiggled his legs nervously. Then he turned suddenly around as if an idea had just occurred to him. "We could meet at that big rock on the nature trail," he said. "We could just be alone while everyone else runs around like crazy people."

"OK." I bit my lip and hesitated only a minute. "I'll meet you there after the game starts."

My fellow Bluebirds were determined to restore the collective honor of all the girls. "The boys beat us at capture the flag," Rachel said, pulling a black sweatshirt over her camp T-shirt. "So they're not going to beat us at mission impossible."

"How does it work, anyway?" I asked, pretending to be interested.

"Jane Richlett is going to hide somewhere with a

bag of tokens," Meghann said. "And we have to go through the dark and find her without getting our arm bands snatched off by the guys' team. The team with the most tokens wins." She looked at me as if something had just occurred to her. "Doug explained all this, Cassie. Weren't you listening?"

I shook my head. Truth was, I was too busy thinking that finally Ethan and I would have a chance to really be alone. Maybe God intended this to be the time when I could talk to him about Jesus Christ. Or maybe Ethan would kiss me again. Either way, being with Ethan was bound to be more exciting than playing mission impossible.

All the other girls put on their grubbies, but I smoothed out my jeans and quietly dabbed a bit of perfume behind my ears, hoping no one would notice. Jane Richlett came in then with our arm bands, and we tied them on each other's upper arms. "The game begins in ten minutes," Jane told us, her eyes sparkling. "Good luck, girls. Don't forget your flashlights!"

We all left the cabin together, but halfway down the road I acted as if I had accidentally forgotten my flashlight. "I'll meet you guys later," I told the other girls. "Don't worry, I'll be fine."

I did go back to my cabin and get my flashlight, but when I headed out again, I walked toward the nature trail. It was a little spooky being in the woods at night, but I made lots of noise with my feet so any lurking animals would hurry away and leave me alone.

My reading rock shone white in the dim moonlight, and it felt cool. It felt a little damp, too, but I sat on it anyway, glad that my jeans were thick enough to keep me from getting really wet. A few minutes passed by, and I began to feel dumb. What if Ethan was out playing the game with his Raccoon buddies? What if this was another one of his mean tricks? Or what if I was attacked by a bear while I was sitting here away from the group? How would I ever explain *that* to anyone?

I heard a twig snap on the path, and I ducked into a shadow, afraid that some kid playing the game had wandered into the woods in search of Jane and her tokens. But it was Ethan. He whispered, "Cassie?" and threw the beam of his flashlight up across his face.

"Do I look scary?" he asked.

"No, you look silly," I said, glad he had come. "Max used to do that all the time—make faces with the flashlight, I mean."

Ethan crept soundlessly over the bushes between the trail and the rock and I noticed how sneaky he could be. "No wonder you're so good at sneaking out at night," I teased him. "How'd you ever learn to walk so quietly through the woods?"

"I read a book about Indians once," Ethan said, settling onto the rock beside me, "and I learned how they could walk through the woods without making a sound. I just practiced until I got it right."

Ethan put his arm around me and I noticed how warm he was compared to the coolness of the rock. "I try to make as much noise as I can," I babbled, rattled by his touch. "To scare away the wild animals, you know."

"Hmmmmm," Ethan looked at me as he spoke, a lazy smile spreading across his face. "You have to watch those wild animals." Then he leaned over and kissed my neck.

His touch tickled, and I cringed involuntarily. He pulled away and looked at me, and I crinkled my nose. "Sorry. That tickled."

"I'm glad you came, Cassie," Ethan said. The moon was behind him, so I couldn't see his face in the darkness, but I knew mine was lit up like a grand opening at the mall. "I think I might be able to believe in you."

"Oh, Ethan, you can believe in me." Didn't my sincerity show on my face? "I want to make you happy."

He took me in his arms then and kissed me.

Chip's kisses had never felt like this. My mind whirled at first like a pinwheel spinning in the wind. Then, after a few minutes, I began to hear Max's voice, over and over: "Your head is on vacation. Your head is on vacation." Max was right. Who could think when they were being kissed like this?

It was getting hard to breathe. Everything inside of me seemed to be tense and on fire. The sound of Ethan's breathing grew uneven, and I felt shivers run through me as one of his hands ran up and down my side, then my arm, then moved toward my front. . . .

Suddenly the pinwheel in my mind stuttered for a minute. Did Ethan know what he was doing? Was this right? What was he doing with his hand? What should I do? Would he think I was a prude if I said something? I couldn't say anything; he was kissing me again. What if I moved his hand? He'd think I was weird or something, wouldn't he?

Ethan groaned and seemed to push his weight on me. I felt myself being lowered onto the rock even as his hand fumbled with a button on my blouse. It was as though I was a tall glass of flaming, mixed-up emotions and the minute he laid me down on the rock, all those emotions spilled out and trickled far away from me.

This wasn't right. I didn't need Max or Jane or

Doug or Chip or anyone else to tell me that this wasn't right. I just knew it.

"No," I said gently, pulling my head away from his. "No, I don't want to do this anymore."

"If you really care about a person, you'll do anything to prove it," Ethan said, not even bothering to look at me as he spoke. He was so confident. Suddenly I felt myself getting angry.

"I won't do anything that's not right," I answered, putting my hands squarely on his shoulders. "Let me up right now, Ethan."

He did look at me then. I thought he was surprised, but it was hard to tell in the dark. "Don't you understand anything?" he said, his tone hard. "If you really want to make me happy, this is the way to do it."

"No way. I have brothers, and I know no guy has ever died because a girl said no. You won't be the first," I snapped. Max would have been proud of me.

"I thought you loved me." His voice was quiet, hurt.

"I told you I cared about you. I do."

"You have a funny way of showing it."

"You have a funny way of asking for it."

Ethan eased up on me then and leaned back on one elbow. "You're living in the dark ages, Cass. Everybody does it these days."

"I'm not everybody."

Ethan wasn't about to give up. I heard him sigh, then he ran his hand slowly down my arm as I struggled to sit up. "I just love you so much, Cassie. You're so different from all the other girls. I just want to give you something special. Don't you want that for us?"

He was about to kiss me again, but I had learned how dangerous those kisses were. "If you want to give me something," I said, moving my head away gently, "give me your respect. And your self-control. I'd appreciate that."

He sat up then and turned his back to me. Suddenly I realized why Max had been so upset with me this afternoon. Even though I hadn't intended to do anything when I agreed to meet Ethan in the woods, still, what would people think if they saw me coming out of the woods with him? Why, they'd think— I shuddered. If Ethan had had his way, they'd have been right. I must have been brain-dead to agree to come here.

I gave Ethan's back a gentle pat.

"It's that Chip guy, isn't it?" he said, turning his face toward me. With his face half-lit by the moonlight, I could see that his eyes were hard. He was angry.

"No, it's not Chip, not really," I said. "I told you

we were just friends, and that's true. But Chip has always treated me with respect. He would never do anything like this."

"Well, that's that." Ethan stood up and brushed off his jeans.

I looked at him, shocked. "You're leaving? Just like that? Aren't we going to talk about—"

"No, Cassie, we're not going to do anything," Ethan said, turning his darkened face in my direction again for a moment. Then he was gone, a soundless shadow in the night. I sat on the rock alone, wanting to go after him, but knowing it would be foolish. *I guess,* I told myself, *our violent fire just burned itself out.*

19

Mission impossible ended shortly after I got back to my cabin, so at least I didn't have to worry about coming in late. "How many tokens did you get, Cassie?" Meghann asked.

"None," I answered truthfully. "I didn't even see Jane Richlett."

"I think the girls won," Rachel said, crawling into her sleeping bag. "And I'm dead tired. G'night, everybody."

Everyone else scrambled around to get ready for bed, and I slipped into the bathroom for a minute of peace. I checked my reflection in the mirror. My eyes looked huge and my skin was pale, but no one could tell from looking at my lips that I'd just been kissing Ethan. And, thankfully, there weren't any marks on my neck or anything. I'd have simply died from embarrassment if that had happened.

I splashed cold water on my face and slipped into my nightgown. Ethan might be mad at me, but I was sure he'd be over it by tomorrow morning. After all, you don't spend days getting to know a girl just to dump her because she won't let you—you know.

Tomorrow I'd wear my cutest outfit and do my hair in a French braid. I'd be pretty and calm, and Ethan would apologize, and he'd never try anything like that again. I had set a good example for him.

I fell asleep knowing that the next morning would be a new start. After all, it was the last day of camp. It simply had to be great.

A car was blowing its horn, and traffic was dead-locked around me. I was standing in the middle of the road in my nightgown thinking, *Why is that car blowing its horn? We're stuck in traffic and blowing the horn won't help.*

Someone shook my shoulder. "Cassie! Wake up! It's the fire alarm!"

It was Jane Richlett, and she dove from bunk to bunk, shaking us out of sleep.

"What a time for a fire drill," murmured Meghann sleepily. "I didn't even bring a robe."

"It's not a drill," Jane said, her voice sharp. "Don't

look for a robe. Get out of bed and get down to the lake, now!"

Meghann, Signe, and Rachel practically fell out of their top bunks while Sondra, Emily, and I jumped out quickly. A fire! A real fire! What on earth?

We joined the fast-moving stream of campers who were jogging toward the lake, and I looked around in the darkness. Fortunately, the full moon had climbed high in the sky, and the white glow from T-shirts and pajamas helped us not to trample each other. There was another light, too, a reddish glow from the boys' cabins.

It was a real fire. The realization hit me as I watched the flames leap from the ground onto a low-hanging limb of a tall pine tree. It raced up the tree like a squirrel.

"Max!" I screamed. "Nick!"

I broke out of the streaming girls and headed toward the ring of boys' cabins. Doug Richlett and several workers of Camp Katumba were there, fighting the fire with blankets and garden hoses.

"Get away from here, girl!" one man shouted as I came near.

"Max!" I screamed, looking for the signs above the doors. Max was in what cabin—the Raccoon? No, that was Nick and Ethan. The Beaver cabin. I looked at the burning cabin. The sign above the door said "Fox."

The Fox cabin! The bullies who had taunted Max and Lincoln and tried to take the Golden Belt of Katumba! Their cabin was on fire!

I ducked behind a tree and watched as the frantic men brought the fire under control. Only one tree had ignited, and it was quickly doused with water from a hose. The front porch and door of the Fox cabin had been badly burned, but the walls were made of cinder block, and fortunately no one had been hurt.

"The boys are all out," I heard a sooty and sweaty man tell Doug Richlett. I recognized his voice—it was Manuel, our trail guide. "They went out the back window when the fire started."

"Let's make sure the fire is all out," Doug said. "Then we'll call the kids back in. We'll have to find a place for the Fox boys to sleep tonight, though."

Kyle Stickle and his cabinmates were standing in a little group with the camp nurse. She was checking them for smoke inhalation, I guess, but apart from being wide-eyed and shivery from the cold and excitement, they were all OK. They looked as bratty as ever.

A fire truck pulled up, its lights flashing red in the darkness, but its sirens off. "We heard you had the fire out," a fireman said as he jumped off the truck. "But we have to make sure. And we have to file a report, of course."

"Paperwork," Doug said, smiling at the fireman. He looked exhausted.

"Yeah, paperwork." The fireman looked at poor Doug. "Buddy, you look like you need to sit down."

"Thanks," Doug said, falling back onto a tree stump. "I do."

Nosy Kyle Stickle came over and stood beside the fireman. "I smelled smoke," he volunteered. "And I woke everybody up."

"Good job," the fireman patted Kyle on the back.

"I also heard a noise," Kyle said. "Someone was on the front porch."

"Really?" The fireman walked around the concrete porch, looking in the muddy water at the charred remains of the front porch railing. Something gleamed through the mud and he bent to pick it up.

"Found something here," he called to Doug. "A gold pen. Engraved with the name 'Thomas Harris, Esquire.' Mean anything to you?"

Doug shook his head, but Kyle stuttered, "It means something to me! It's that Max Perkins kid. That's his pen! I saw him writing with it the other day!"

The fireman flattened his lips and put the pen

into a plastic bag. "Better check with that Perkins kid," he told Doug. "Find out why he'd want to set fire to this cabin."

"He hates us, that's why," Kyle said. "He's a weirdo anyway."

From behind the tree, I sank down, my back rubbing against the tree's rough bark. Max couldn't have set that fire. Not even accidentally. But I knew someone else who had a Thomas Harris pen, my pen. Ethan. And he had promised to take care of the boys in the Fox cabin for me.

I slipped away from the cabins through the trees until I met the campers coming back up along the road. I dodged through the group until I met Max. Lincoln was with him.

"Max, quick," I pulled him out of the crowd and off the road. "Where's your gold pen? The one with Tom's name on it?"

Max looked at me as if I had lost my marbles. "I don't know. I think I lost it in the lake the day Kyle and his buddies flipped our canoe. Why?"

"Because someone set a fire outside the Fox cabin and dropped a Thomas Harris pen there, that's why."

Max whistled.

"That's not all. Kyle Stickle told Doug and the fireman that you have it in for them or something."

Lincoln snickered. "That's silly. They wanted to get *us*. We never did anything to them."

Max was thinking, and he looked at me. "Did you bring a pen from home?"

I looked away. I didn't want him to know about Ethan.

"Maybe. If I did, I haven't seen it in a couple of days." That much was true.

Max looked perturbed, but he just started walking back up the cabin road. "We'll have to prove our alibi, Lincoln."

"We?"

"Yes, *we*. You don't think they'll blame me alone, do you? You're the one with the Golden Belt of Katumba, and that's what the Fox boys want."

Lincoln realized what Max was saying. "We were in bed asleep, though. How can we prove that? Everyone was asleep."

"Everyone but one person," Max said, his eyes serious. But he smiled at me. "Don't worry, Cassie. I'll figure this one out."

20

I don't know how anyone expected us to go back to sleep after that. It was four-thirty by my watch by the time we got back to our cabin, and we shivered under our sleeping bags. The night air was cool, plus we were excited.

"Did you see that good-looking fireman with the beard?" Meghann asked, peeping out from under her sleeping bag. "He was really fine!"

"My mother won't believe this," Rachel said. "She will probably never let me come back to camp again."

"How did it start, anyway?" Emily wanted to know. "There was no lightning. Was someone play-ing with matches?"

"At three in the morning?" Signe asked. "Not likely."

"No one knows," I muttered. "We may never know."

After an hour or so, I could hear the gentle breathing of the other girls and I knew they had at last gone back to sleep. But it was out of the question for me. I knew Ethan had set that fire. I couldn't prove it, of course, but I knew it. But why had he done it? Was it to prove something to me or was he just mad? Had he dropped my pen on purpose? Why? To make Max look guilty? No, he didn't even know Max had a pen like mine. Would he want to frame me?

Ethan was sitting with Nick and the other guys from the Raccoon cabin the next morning at breakfast. He hadn't saved me a seat, but maybe he knew we girls would oversleep. We were up late last night.

"I need to talk to you," I told him, feeling a strange sense of déjà vu.

"Going to preach at me again?" he asked, his eyes gleaming. "What's it about this time, Cass?"

"In private. I'll meet you after breakfast."

I sat with the girls in my cabin, who seemed surprised to see me but didn't say anything. And after breakfast, I walked up to Ethan and pulled him away from his friends.

"I need my pen back," I said, trying to be casual. "My Thomas Harris pen, remember?"

"That pen?" Ethan's expression was blank. "I don't know where it is. I think I lost it."

"It's a funny thing," I said, "they found one just like it last night at the Fox cabin. In the ashes. They think whoever set the fire dropped it there."

Ethan looked startled for a minute, then he tossed his head back defiantly. "Why would anyone do that?"

"That's what I'd like to know."

"Maybe someone was getting even with those brats." Ethan looked up at me and smiled as calmly as if he were discussing the weather. "Maybe someone was trying to prove something. What does it matter? Camp is over tomorrow anyway, and they can't do anything to anyone. Don't worry about it, pretty lady."

He walked away then, whistling, and I walked down to the lake to sit and think. If Ethan had set the fire to prove something to me, it was wrong and he was crazy. But what could I do about it? There was no way I could help him if I turned him in and Doug sent him home. Plus, if I turned him in, he'd not only be disappointed in me, he'd hate my guts forever. For sure.

I sat down on the diving dock and propped my head on my knees. How could Ethan be so charming and witty and dangerous all at once? And why did I still feel attracted to him?

Later that afternoon Ethan found me by the lake, reading. He'd been playing basketball, and he and Nick were both dripping with sweat. "Hey, Cass, there's a hayride and bonfire tonight," Ethan said, smiling widely. "You still want to go with me?"

"Sure," I said, but without much enthusiasm. "I'll be there."

Ethan grinned at Nick. "She's cute," he said, jerking his thumb at me. "Where'd you find her?"

Nick rolled his eyes. "You can have her," he mumbled.

I was tempted to ask Nick if he'd noticed whether or not Ethan had slipped out last night, but I decided against it. I'd seen how quiet Ethan could be when he wanted to sneak around, and it was probably better to forget about the fire. The damage didn't look so bad in the morning, anyway. The beams from the front porch were charred, and one tree was blackened, but the fire marshal said whoever started the fire apparently had just built a little fire on the porch to scare the kids inside. It just got out of hand because things were so dry.

I closed my book and started back to the cabin when I saw Doug Richlett walking along the cabin road. Doug was carrying the Golden Belt of Katumba.

"Don't tell me you guessed the riddle," I teased him. "That's not fair. You made this whole thing up."

Doug shook his head. "No. I've had to call the whole thing off. Since Max and Lincoln probably started that fire, I just can't let them win the prize for the belt. The Fox cabin was in second place, so they can have the party."

"But they didn't start the fire!" I protested. "I asked Max!"

Doug's eyes were patient. "Cassie, Kyle Stickle says he saw Max using the pen that was found in the ashes."

"Maybe he dropped it there earlier."

"No way. The fire marshal said it would have been buried under the mud if it hadn't been dropped on top of the wood used to start the fire."

"But that's circumstantial evidence. That's not fair."

Doug shook his head. "I'm sorry, Cassie, but that's all I've got. Right now everything points to Max. I'm not convicting him, I'm just not letting him win the prize. The other kids would have a fit if I let Max's cabin have a party if they were the ones who set the fire."

I shut my mouth and Doug walked away, carrying the precious golden belt. Max and Lincoln had worked all week for nothing. They were being blamed for something they didn't do. I had to make a decision about whether or not to let things remain the way they were.

On the one hand, I told myself, it was no big deal that Max and Lincoln wouldn't get their precious party. What was a party, after all? Because if I told Doug about Ethan, Ethan would hate me. He might get into serious trouble. Besides, I couldn't prove that Ethan even did it—I had only my suspicions.

On the other hand, I knew Max and Lincoln had nothing to do with the fire. They had worked hard to win that dumb party, and it wasn't fair that everyone in camp now thought they were arsonists. And Max was my brother—wasn't I supposed to be loyal to my brother? If Ethan did set the fire, he should be held responsible.

I couldn't go behind Ethan's back and rat on him. So right after dinner I found him and pulled him aside. "I'm going to tell Doug Richlett that you had my gold pen," I said calmly, watching his eyes. "I'm not doing it to get you in trouble, Ethan, I just want everyone to know Max didn't set that fire."

"So you'll blame it on me?" Ethan's voice was cool.

"No, I'm not blaming it on anyone," I said. "I just want the entire truth to come out."

Ethan whirled away from me then and turned his temper on a small tree nearby. With three quick chops, he broke three low branches off the tree. "Sometimes I hate you church people," he snapped, turning back around to look at me. "You say you care, but you don't. You'd sacrifice me to save your egghead little brother, wouldn't you? What's with you, girl? I thought you wanted someone to take care of those brats in the Fox cabin, but when—"

"Stop!" I covered my ears with my hands. I didn't want to hear any more. "I didn't ask you to burn down the cabin!" I whispered intensely. "Someone could have been killed!"

Ethan shook his head, and there was something in his eyes: hurt, rebellion, pain. "I can't believe you," he said. "I don't understand you at all."

"You can be so stupid!" I screamed at him, not caring who heard. "So mean, and so dumb, and—you just don't think, do you, Ethan?"

"I don't have to listen to this," Ethan said, turning away. "I hate everyone in this entire stinkin' place."

Ethan didn't sit with me in the service, of course. I didn't have a chance to tell Doug my suspicions about the fire. At the hayride, Ethan and Nick climbed aboard one of the wagons and sat in the back. Ethan was in a dark, gloomy mood, and Nick seemed bewildered. He didn't know what was going on.

Meghann and the other girls kept whispering

"What happened?" when they saw Ethan and me apart, but I just smiled and shook my head. They'd have to keep wondering.

Poor Max and Lincoln were shunned by everyone. The Fox boys loved it and did a good job of making sure everyone thought Max and Lincoln were flaming weirdos. Dejected, they climbed into the first hay wagon; Nick and Ethan were in the last one. My fellow Bluebirds and I rode in the wagon with Nick and Ethan.

When we arrived at the clearing for the bonfire, we climbed out of the wagons and circled the large pile of wood. We sat in the grass as Doug lit the fire, and I was uncomfortable at seeing the bright flames. This fire was carefully controlled, but it still felt strange looking at flames when last night they had been leaping up a tree not fifty feet away from me.

The fire was obviously on Doug's mind, too. "Look at this fire," he told us. "This bonfire is for our good use," he said, holding his hands up to the blaze. "This fire warms us. Later we will roast marshmallows in it. It has a purpose. It is, in its own way, very beautiful."

He turned his back to the fire and looked at us circled around him. "Last night's fire was not for a good use," he said simply. "It had no purpose. It was destructive. Left to itself, it would have destroyed everything in its path. It was uncontrolled, and it could have brought death to this beautiful place."

The twigs on the bonfire sizzled and popped as Doug looked at us. Ethan and Nick were seated in the circle across from me, and I could see their faces in the golden glow of the flames. Nick was listening carefully to Doug; Ethan was watching the campfire.

"There is a spirit in each of you that is like a fire," Doug said. "If you let that flaming spirit run unchecked and uncontrolled, it can bring destruction and death. But if you submit your spirit and life to God, *and let him control it,* your life will have a purpose. It will be beautiful."

Doug turned around and watched the fire dance. Sparks flew into the blackness of the air, red-hot sizzlers that danced in the hot breeze of the fire. "Does anyone have anything to say?" Doug asked, looking around at us. "What have you learned at camp this week?"

There was an awkward silence as each of us waited for someone else to speak. Then a boy got up and shared something, then another girl. Other kids rose to their feet and said what they'd learned about discovering God's will, and suddenly I knew that this was the time and place for me to do something. It was an answer to my prayer.

I stood up and cleared my throat. A sea of faces

turned toward me and I felt my knees grow a little weak. "I have something to say about last night's fire," I began. I glanced over at Nick and Ethan in time to see Ethan angrily kick the ground.

I looked back at Doug. "I want you all to know that my brother Max couldn't have set that fire," I said. "Even though a pen like his was found there. I have a pen like that one, too, and Max and I both lost our pens this week."

There was a gentle stir among the circle, but I saw Max's eyes shining toward me in gratitude. "So anyone could have found one of our pens and used it this week. Anyone at all. That's all I want to say."

I sat down abruptly, and I could feel Ethan staring at me from across the flames. He probably thought I didn't rat on him because I was madly in love with him or something, but that wasn't the reason at all. I cared about Ethan, I really did, but I had been stupid to think he needed my help. He needed a lot more than I could give. Like last night's runaway fire, Ethan needed to get his life under control.

Doug scratched his head and thanked me for speaking. "Thank you, Cassie," he said slowly, "And I hope whoever set that fire will deal with their own conscience and God. I hope someone will come and tell me the truth. Until then, I'm not going to penalize the Beaver cabin unfairly. They won the Golden

Belt of Katumba, and they can have the party they deserve."

The Beaver cabin roared their approval, and I was glad. Our serious mood was broken, so Doug held up a bag of marshmallows and a handful of palmetto stems. "Everybody grab a marshmallow and a stick," he said, grinning. "Remember, I like mine crispy and burnt."

During the hayride back to the cabins, most of us sang songs until we were hoarse. Ethan sat over in the corner of the wagon, staring out across the dark landscape, and Nick actually came and sat by me.

"Hey, Nick," I said, flicking his arm with a piece of straw. "Remember when you told Uncle Jacob you were tired of being a gentleman?"

Nick nodded. "Yeah."

"I said you were boring. Remember?"

"How can I forget?" Nick smiled at me, and I felt bad *again* for saying it.

"Stay just the way you are, Nick. That girl Jacklyn may not appreciate you, but I do."

Nick looked away for a minute, then he grabbed a handful of straw and lazily tossed it in my hair. "You've thought about a lot this week, huh?"

"Yeah." I laughed. "A lot." I grabbed a handful of straw and was about to stuff it down the front of his shirt when I noticed two gold pens in his shirt pocket.

"Are those Tom's pens? Did you bring them both from home?"

Puzzled, Nick pulled them out of his pocket. "No, I only brought one. I found the other one on the floor of our cabin." He shrugged. "I guess Ethan dropped it."

Ethan dropped his pen in the cabin—he couldn't have dropped it at the scene of the fire! Ethan didn't set the fire!

I leaned back against the side of the wagon, my mouth open. Then who set the fire? It wasn't Max, because his pen was lost the day Kyle Stickle and the boys dumped his canoe. I suddenly remembered something—Kyle Stickle in the cafeteria, telling Max, "Enjoy it while you can, bud, because you're not winning any party."

Could Kyle possibly have set the fire outside his own cabin and planted Max's pen to make sure Max and his cabin didn't win the party? It was possible. The more I thought about it, it was logical, too.

"I think I know who set the fire," I told Nick.

"Don't worry about it," Nick said. "If you can't prove it, you have no case."

Good grief, Nick sounded more like Tom the lawyer every day. I shut up and leaned back against the itchy straw to think. Whoever set the fire, it wasn't Ethan. He must think I was really terrible to accuse him.

As we unloaded from the wagons, I congratulated Max and Lincoln on winning the party for their cabin. "By the way, what was the answer to that riddle?" I asked Max. "You can tell me now."

"What walks on four legs in the morning, two legs at noon, and three legs in the evening?" Max said. "A man, of course. Babies, in the 'morning' of life, crawl on four legs, mature men walk on two, and in the 'evening' of life old men walk on three legs."

"Three legs?" I crinkled my nose. "I don't get it."

"They use a cane!" Lincoln exclaimed triumphantly, ready to bolt for the rec room where they were having their party.

"One more thing," I grabbed Lincoln's shirt before he got away. "Do you still think that belt was lucky?"

Lincoln smiled. "No way," he said, laughing a little. "It brought me more trouble than anything. Winning the party had nothing to do with luck. It's only because you said something, Cassie, that we're winners tonight."

I let him go, and Lincoln and Max ran to their party. I walked alone in the dark down the road to my cabin. Ethan was waiting at the fork in the road.

I stopped in front of him and looked up. This time it was his face in the moonlight; mine was in shadow.

"You didn't say anything about me," he said simply. "I was surprised. I get blamed for everything."

"No, I didn't," I said, shaking my head. "I know you didn't do it, Ethan. I'm sorry for accusing you."

Ethan shrugged. His face was calm in the moonlight, like a child's. The mischievous sparkle was gone. He reached for my hand, and I moved it away, hugging my own arms tightly. "I'm chilly," I whispered, a feeble excuse.

Ethan put his hands in his pockets and looked down at me, a puzzled look on his face. "I don't understand you people," he said finally. "I really don't. I've never known a girl like you, Cassie."

I smiled at him, feeling strangely confident. I'd never been confident around Ethan, but this time I was sure I had done something right. "I wish you the very best in everything," I told him. "And I hope you find what you really need, even though I don't think it's what you're looking for."

Ethan was still puzzled, but he shook his head. He looked so handsome, so confused, that I wanted to hug him—but I just smiled and stepped past him. "You're something special, Ethan, to me and to God. Never forget that."

I had gone only two steps when I heard him call, "Will I see you again?"

I doubted it, but he was Nick's friend, after all. "Maybe . . . ," I called over my shoulder, not daring to look back at him. "When the fire's under control."

It was time for lights out, so I walked on to my cabin and started to pack my suitcase in the dark. Tomorrow we'd have a long drive home.